Parvati: February

Mystic Zodiac

Book 2

Brandy Walker

Parvati: February, Mystic Zodiac
Copyright © 2015 Brandy Walker
Cover by TEZ Graphics, Brandy Walker
Image: © Arminaudovenko | Dreamstime.com
Image: © Starblue | Dreamstime.com
Edited by Noel Varner

First Electronic Print, Feb 2015

QUOTE:

I'm a successful, beautiful woman providing love to the World. That should be enough…shouldn't it? ~ Parvati

BLURB:

Parvati Shiva, a true descendent of the Goddess of love and devotion, is fed up. She runs a successful dating site, connecting Mystics and humans all over the world with their one true love. The only she hasn't been able to find love for is…her.

When a hacker gets into her network and website, shutting down her site in the height of the busy season, she calls on her cousin Jag for help, who in turn reaches out to an old friend.

Colin Patterson, IT guru and confirmed bachelor, quickly agrees to help his friend's sister out with her computer problem, hoping it will be a long drawn out process. He's eager to escape his mother's matchmaking Valentine's Day party. She's invited all of the single women — and a few men — to jump-start his dating life, something he has no interest in at all.

One mistaken identity later, Colin ruins his chance with the beautiful Indian woman he's instantly attracted to. Will he be able to prove he isn't a boss bashing idiot, save Parvati's company, and win her affections before he doesn't have a reason to stick around?

Warning: This book contains a geeky hero who can't keep his mouth shut, a strong willed businesswoman dealing in love, and an attraction that neither can deny.

Please note: This book has a hot M/M scene.

Mystic Zodiac: Parvati

PROLOGUE

Chloe paced the ornate oriental rugs strewn about Eros's living room, the soft padding under her feet made her want to kick her slippers off and curl her toes in. Making herself at home wasn't on the agenda. It had been five minutes since she'd arrived. The servant girl who let her in warned Chloe it would be a couple of minutes before Eros could join her, but that didn't stop her mood from souring.

He's probably screwing some other woman right now! Not that she had a claim on the man, but that was beside the point. He knew she would be arriving and the time. She'd sent a missive just that morning to ensure he knew exactly when to expect her. The fact that he didn't have the consideration to be available when she showed up stoked the ire bubbling within. There was no reason he couldn't have told her the night before about the next couple. Saying he had only gone to the Turning Ceremony to take part in the festivities wasn't reason enough not to discuss the task.

Take your mind off what he might be doing you fool. Chastising herself, she focused on her surroundings. She needed something to take her mind off him; maybe she would find something of significance to use against him. Something to force his hand in their little bet.

No, she wouldn't use that tasty nugget about using the Grigori and Eternal for their first challenge. While she didn't mind seeing him being blasted by Zeus, she didn't want their game to end, which is exactly what would happen. Zeus's temper, when it came to the things he considered his and his alone, could be — bothersome.

The low-slung furniture in cool shades of brown, and the minimal decoration, were not at all how she pictured Eros living. In her mind, she imagined dim lighting, plush surfaces, and the place reeking of sex and sin: the perfect setting for debauching some young maiden or desperate Goddess. A veritable den of iniquity.

The pretty little thing, the same one that answered the door, came into the room. She giggled and kept her head down, as she brought in a tray with a decanter of mead and two empty goblets. She dropped cinnamon sticks into each cup, before filling them with the steaming drink. She motioned to the couch; but Chloe declined, shaking her head sharply. She did, however, take the goblet from the girl and send her away before she silenced the girl's incessant laughter with a slap.

Chloe was not in Eros's home to relax or let her guard down, as much as she longed to do just that. He would take advantage given the chance and change the terms of the agreement. She had a sneaky suspicion he would play with her emotionally. Make her believe he wanted her, then leave her wanting.

After his visit to her home the previous month, she was left with a pulsing need to be filled. To have his cock drill into her from behind. She'd been forced to take matters into her own hands in hopes of sating the need he'd left boiling in her. She had been unable to play with one of her usual consorts, and cried out in frustration when pleasuring herself did nothing to help. In fact, as she lay on her bed panting after her release, her body ached even more for his touch.

"That will not happen this time," she murmured. Wildly, she looked around for something to capture her attention.

A picture hanging over the couch did the trick. There was nothing stunning or awe inspiring about it. It was a view of the landscape in which they lived. Nothing she couldn't see on a daily basis by simply walking out her front door. The image, though, drew her in as if she'd been ensnared by magic. It gave her something to focus on other than the delectable man she waited for. Leaning toward the picture, she noticed in the corner, on a field of grass, a young man lay entwined with a woman. They were having sex. The legs of the woman were wrapped around his lean waist. The golden head of the man was tossed back in ecstasy. It looked very similar to Eros's visage; and the woman, though she couldn't see the face, had long brown hair like her own. Chloe shuddered, imagining being in that position with him.

She sucked in a shocked breath when the image took life the longer she stared. He slid forward, thrusting his pelvis against the woman's. She arched beneath him and threw her hands above her head. The male figure grasped her wrists, locking her in place. Without thought, Chloe rubbed her own, wondering how it would feel…the pressure, the inability to touch back. Her core throbbed in anticipation.

"Are you ready for the next couple?" Eros whispered in her ear.

Chloe startled. He had entered the room and walked up behind her without notice. As much as she tried, she couldn't suppress the faint tremor that took hold of her body. Nor could she stop the image of him pushing her forward, making her brace herself on the back of the couch, so he could take her from behind. With a flick of his wrist, he could have her chiton out of the way and have his wicked way with her.

She'd taken a page from his book, wanting to torture him as he tormented her. Before coming to his place, she'd found her shortest and tightest outfit. The dark blue garment cupped her breasts lovingly and barely covered her ass, but it left a lot to be desired in the warmth department.

Taking a steadying breath, she spun on her heel and came face-to-face with the man occupying her thoughts. Eros, as usual, was barely dressed.

Did he do that for her? Letting her see what she desired but was denied. Did he enjoy tormenting and teasing her? Or had it been because he was overheated from a bout of sex with some nameless, faceless nymph that would flit off to find another man to seduce?

She leisurely glanced at his body, taking note of the lack of perspiration on his golden skin. His cheeks weren't flushed, and he wasn't breathing heavy.

No, he had not been with another woman while she waited for him. He had deliberately made her wait, but to what end.

She would not take the bait, if that had been his tactic. Raising the goblet to her lips, she sipped the hot drink. It slid down her throat, warming her up from the inside, causing her to moan loudly. She did not realize how cold she was until that moment. Her nipples puckered as the chill chased through her blood. Her toes curled in her slippers.

Eros took the drink from her hand and set it down behind him. He inched forward, allowing his glorious bare chest to brush against her. The warm scent of man wafted around her, and she almost sighed. Hold it together!

"Your cheeks have turned the most alluring shade of pink, my sweet, Chloe. I wonder, is it from the mead or from my proximity to you?"

Chloe huffed out a breath, covering up the truth of what he said. "Do not think I am so easily aroused by your appearance, Eros. The mead is hot and the day quite cool. My reaction is merely a result of the two."

"Maybe you should have put more clothing on then." His gaze raked her up and down. The visual caress making her core clench. The corner of his mouth twitched as if suppressing a smile, knowing the affect he had on her.

The urge to punch him in the face passed through her like lightening on a wire and had her fingers flexing. "My clothing and how I dress is none of your concern. I am fine now that I've had the hot mead." He stared at her expectantly. She wasn't completely without manners. "Thank you."

He snorted in response. "If you say so."

"If we can get down to business," she said through gritted teeth.

"Still eager to be beneath me, Chloe? Do you want me to hold your wrists down like in the painting? Do you want to be helpless in my arms? Allow me to do as I please with your body?"

Clenching her jaw tightly, so no words could fly out of her mouth, she stared at him mutinously.

Eros sighed deeply and took a step back. "Since you are not in the mood to play, let's discuss the challenge."

"Yes, let's do that now, since you would not the night before." She skirted around him and sat on a nearby chair. It would prevent him from touching her, and her from grabbing onto him like she desired. Today was about a battle of wills, not bodies. He tempted her too much, and she had an idea he knew it. There was no need to further enhance his knowledge of that.

Leaning back, she adopted an air of nonchalance. "Are you saying there will be a challenge at some point? As you witnessed last night, matching up the Grigori and the

Eternal was entirely too easy."

Eros shrugged and sprawled on the couch. His bare chest was highlighted in a beam of sunlight streaming into the room. The thin cloth wrapped around his waist had edged up, and she wondered if she would get a peek at his nether region. It was surely short enough that she could, if only he would turn his legs a bit more her way.

"… ease you into things."

Chloe forced herself to look into his face. She had missed the beginning of what he said, so she took an educated guess. "Really? I find that hard to believe. Making things difficult is second nature to you."

"There's still plenty of time for that. You do have eleven more couples." Eros tapped his fingers against his leg. Her gazed snagged on the movement. She would love to run her hands up his solid thighs and feel their strength. Search out his cock and balls to gently fondle until he was hard and mad with need.

"…a lesser Goddess." Enthralled with his body, Chloe found she was, yet again, left guessing as to what he talked about.

"A lesser Goddess? That will be easy as well. I thought you said there would be a challenge at some point."

"And I wondered if you were even paying attention. Are you that distracted by me, Chloe? Should I summon a servant and have her bring me more clothing?"

She rolled her eyes at his preposterousness. It was the only alternative to screaming no and begging him to take the rest off. "There is no need for you to cover up, Eros. I am not that taken with you. Your body intrigues me, that is all."

Eros snorted. "No. I believe it more than intrigues you. I inflame you, my sweet Chloe. Your nipples are beaded and arousal colors your cheeks. Blame the mead if you want, but I know the truth. You want me with every fiber of your being, or you wouldn't be here playing this little game. Admit it, you want me and would do anything to have me."

He was right, but there was no need to tell him. She still felt the need to be aloof. To act as if this bet didn't matter to her, if only to save her pride.

Over the past month, she had done nothing but lust after him. Dream of him. Look for him when she was out. Images of his naked body haunted her at every corner. His body a playground she wanted desperately to explore.

She forced a lighthearted chuckle out. "This bet means nothing to me. Owing you a favor would not kill me. I am amused you think so. You are nothing but a hot piece of ass I want for a small amount of time. If it doesn't happen it won't be the end of my world. Someone else will come along that catches my fancy and beg to be my toy."

Eros flinched fractionally as the hurtful words spewed from her mouth. She would have missed it if she hadn't been watching closely for a reaction. She was being crass and downplaying how much she wanted to crawl over to him and beg for the pleasure he promised with one dark look. Only pleasure wasn't what she was seeing in his eyes now.

They were narrowed, and she felt the look he passed over her body again. It was another heated caress that made her pussy cream. When his gaze lingered on her breasts, before tracking back to her face, she was forced to sit still. Act as though it did nothing to her. Inside she squirmed to feel his physical touch. Could imagine his large hands drifting down to her breasts, where he would pluck and tease the already hard points.

He crossed his impressive arms over his chest, as a smile cocked up one side of his mouth. "I do not believe you, but will let that go for now. I think it best to get on with things. The female for this month's fun and games is one of my own. Parvati is a lesser Goddess of love and devotion. She yearns to find the man she will fall in love with and who will be hers through eternity. As I am pleased with all she has done for me, I have decided it is time to grant her wish. She is fated to fall in love with a human named Colin."

Chloe waited for more, but realized he would not be any more forthcoming. "Nothing else?"

Eros stood. "No. As I told you before, I will only give you the names. The rest is up to you." He stood and stared down at her. "We will meet at the Parthenon next time."

Surprise at his words stole her breath. Had she pushed him too far with her declaration? Chloe stood and faced him, not willing to let on that she was frightened she had ruined things. "Afraid to be alone with me, Eros?" She sassed.

"No, but I have decided we need witnesses to this bet. That's how it started and how it shall end. I wouldn't want you to cry foul when you don't succeed."

Her head came up a notch, and she did her damnedest to look down her nose at him. Hard to do when he towered over her. "A Goddess of love and devotion is not going to turn down love. She will jump at the chance when it is presented to her. You should have given me a better couple."

"A human is more complex than you assume, Chloe. This will be plenty challenging for you. And, I won't change my mind about the Parthenon. An audience would be best suited to future meetings."

She noticed his tightly clenched fists by his sides, and secretly knew there was more to it than that. Conceding, for now, was the best move for her. "As you wish. I will see you at the beginning of March. Your goddess and her human won't know what hit them."

*****

Eros watched as Chloe strode out his front door. "A hot piece of ass," he mumbled after the door slammed shut. He was more than that, and he would have her on her knees apologizing for that remark. "She will beg for forgiveness."

Storming into his bedroom, he flung himself on his bed. Childish, he knew, but what else was he supposed to do? The second those words were out of her mouth; he wanted to demand she take them back. Demand she tell him the truth, which was that she loved verbally sparring with him almost as much as she desired his body. That it built the rising tension between them.

She would come to regret those words when they met next. He would make sure of it.

CHAPTER ONE

February 2nd – Morning 900

"No, no, no!" Parvati smashed the keys on her keyboard; hoping one of them would stop the pop-ups decorating her screen. Her computer display froze for a second before a new single box popped up in the middle. "You're drunk. Go home. No one wants to date you." The giant laughing emoticon that followed filling up the screen pushed her over the edge. Picking up her mouse, she threw it across the room, watching with no sense of satisfaction as it pinged off the wall.

Why couldn't that have made her feel better? "Fucking technology," she growled. Not that she didn't love all things techie; she did, just not at the moment.

Stacy, her assistant, poked her head into the room. "I see you've found out." She squeezed through the barely open door, hands clasped in front of her demurely. She chewed on her lips nervously, and Parvati knew right then she wasn't going to like what would come out of Stacy's mouth.

"Why didn't you tell me when I walked in this

morning?" She knew she sounded whiney but didn't care. This was the last thing she needed at the moment.

"I wasn't aware of the problem until Jag called."

Squeezing her eyes shut tight, Parvati counted back from ten.

10…

9…

8…

She would have put her hands over her ears to keep from hearing anything, but that would have been childish and not the behavior of the head of a thriving Internet dating company.

7…

6…slowly breathe in and out. Find your center. Her therapist's voice echoed words of advice in her head. The soothing tone doing nothing for her at the moment.

"We've been hacked. At least that's what Jag says. He told me to tell you he's bringing someone in to help find, fix, and contain the problem. He's not sure when that will be though. He has to get hold of the whoever this technical guru is and see if he's free first."

Stacy's words jolted her from her countdown. Her therapist told her it would help her relax and think clearly. Boy was she wrong. That bitch wasn't getting her repeat business.

Parvati groaned and dropped her head to the keyboard in defeat, banging it lightly. One more thing to go wrong that day—she should have just stayed in bed. It started shitty and looked like it would end shitty.

Mother-fuck!

When the heel on her favorite pair of shoes snapped as she walked out her front door, she should have just turned around, stripped naked, and crawled back under the covers until the day came to an end.

Nope. Not her. Not Ms. I-have-to-impress-the-boss-or-he'll-fire-me. She trudged on even though she had an inkling things wouldn't get better. She tossed the shoes and grabbed another pair. Luckily, she made it to her favorite teashop without incident. Unluckily for her, her tea got knocked over before she even had a chance to take a sip. The busy mom with the three rambunctious kids bumping into her as she walked out the teashop door.

To top off her morning, the asshat she went on a blind date with earlier in the month hand-delivered a wedding invitation, and thanked her for proving the gossip right.

Now there was…THIS. Hacked! Who would want to hack a dating website? She knew the answer before she even finished the thought. A supremely disgruntled customer or rejected suitor. The ratio of displeased customers and suitors was minimal when compared to happy clients. But the rejects — they were really unhappy. Hate mail. Social media bashing. Failed cyber attacks. Unfortunately, in this business, there would always be a match that didn't work out, and they would always have to deal with the aftermath. This time, Parvati wasn't sure she could handle it.

Stacy's voice filtered through the myriad of thoughts circling in her head.

"Sweetie, you might want to stop that or the space bar will be permanently etched into your forehead. How would that go over on your date tonight?"

Parvati groaned even louder, but stopped bouncing her head off the keyboard. She'd forgotten about the blind date she was supposed to go on that evening. Seriously, what was the use? They never panned out. She was forever saddled with men finding their soul mates while out with her. As a Goddess of love and devotion, it would have been fantastic if it happened through one of the matches. But, as a woman who wanted to find the love of her life, well, it blew chunks.

Lifting her head, she sighed in resignation. "I'm going to have to cancel. It isn't like the date would work out anyway. I think the guys are catching on that they'll find their soul mate if they date me. The last guy I went out with spent the entire time searching the restaurant for someone else. He handed me his wedding invitation just this morning."

Stacy strode across the room in her impossibly high stilettos and planted herself next to Parvati. The pixie-like woman's dark eyebrows drew down in worry. "Ah, sweetie, that sucks. But maybe this guy is the one. He is pretty yummy looking and an engineer. Beauty and brains to match yours. Just the way you like them."

Parvati snorted and sat up straight. "Aren't they all? Hot engineers seem to be a dime a dozen these days. Maybe I need to start looking elsewhere. I could try out a corporate lawyer."

Stacy's nose wrinkled in disgust. "You hate lawyers. Too full of themselves. What about a college professor? You dig the nerdy type. A tweed jacket and crooked glasses, and you'd be putty in his hands. The only downfall is I'm not sure he'd know what to do with you once he got you naked."

Parvati resisted the urge to bash her head against the keyboard again. "Intelligence is sexy and totally my kryptonite. No! I need to cancel. If we don't get this hacker problem fixed before Valentine's Day, we're screwed. That's our biggest holiday; when we get the most hits and matches. I can't go back to the big boss and tell him 'sorry, maybe next time.' You know he expects results. Also, people are more open to finding love right now. Valentine's Day is magical and people want a sparkle of it in their life."

Stacy perched her pert ass on the desk. "Yeah, I know. I just hate to see you down about dating. It doesn't look good when our boss hates on love. Maybe you can meet up with…Greg?"

"Gordon," Parvati said, her voice devoid of emotion. That right there told her she wasn't interested in the guy. If she couldn't be excited when she talked about going on a date with him, she shouldn't bother going. It would be a waste of time for both of them.

"Sure, Gordon. Whatever. You need to take the edge off, girlfriend. Call him up and say you only have time for a quickie. I doubt Greg…"

"Gordon."

Stacy waved her hand dismissively. "It doesn't matter what his name is because I doubt he'd care what you called him as long as your long, toned legs were wrapped around his waist. Just call out 'oh stud' every once in a while and moan really loud. You can even do it here, and I won't breath a word or let anyone near your office."

"You're such a perv. You just want to sit and listen." Parvati laughed, and some of the tension in her shoulders finally released.

Stacy shrugged. "Eh, you know you love that about me. What else are BFF's for anyway?"

The phone in the outer office started to ring, grabbing their attention. Stacy hopped off the desk. "Gotta run. The boss will kill me if she knows I've been trying to get her laid." She stuck her tongue out at Parvati and practically ran from the office.

Parvati rolled her eyes and snatched up her own phone. She needed to know exactly what was going on, and the only one who could tell her was her cousin Jag, her head IT guru.

CHAPTER TWO

February 2nd – Morning, sometime after 10am

Jagjit, better known as Jag, picked up the phone on the fourth ring. He knew exactly who was calling him, and he couldn't help but torment her. There were times Parvati had a stick shoved so far up her butt, he didn't think it had a chance in hell at being removed. "Jag speaking," he said casually, kicking his feet up on his desk.

"Fours rings," she screeched over the line, forcing him to pull it away from his ear. "Do you understand how big of a mess this is, Jag? The whole company is fucked at the moment, and you're taking your time answering the damn phone when you knew damn well I would be calling."

He waited a heartbeat more to make sure the yelling stopped. He placed the phone back up to his ear. "I think you're being a bit dramatic. Didn't your therapist tell you to work on calming down? I'm pretty certain you told me it would help with those stress headaches you get. And I wouldn't say the whole company is fucked, only a little messed up at the moment."

"Argh! Don't fuck with me Jag. Not right now. Our

entire season is at stake."

"We have a season?" He laughed into the receiver, thinking it was a joke but knowing Parvati, she was completely serious. Leave it to his uptight cousin to actually think like that. Love didn't happen one month, hell — one day — out of the year. You would think a Goddess of love and devotion would know that.

He heard her pouting on the other end. Could imagine her mouth turned down and arms crossed over her chest. He'd seen it regularly growing up. "You know what I mean."

"I'm sorry, Vati." And he was. He knew the company meant the world to her. He just wished she'd lighten up some. Or get laid.

When her voice came back over the line, it was calm and steady, just like he was used to. "How bad is it? Can it be fixed by COB today?"

"COB?" He chuckled softly. The woman was forever using acronyms for things. There were times he needed a cheat sheet just to figure out what the hell she was talking about.

"Close of business," she said exasperated. "Why do you always act like you don't know what I'm talking about?"

"Because I know it irritates you." When would she ever learn? He loved winding her up. It's what family did. The fact they grew up together and were the same age played into it too. She was like a sister to him.

"Good to know," she snorted.

"Have you really calmed down now?"

She exhaled noisily. "As much as I can at the moment."

"Good. I hate it when you get like this."

"Then don't make it worse by dragging it out," she

pleaded. "Give it to me straight."

Jag's grin fell away. She wasn't going to like what he had to say, which was why he was picking on her. "Okay. We've been hacked. So far everything we've tried hasn't worked. I can't fix it."

"What?" she shouted before he could tell her anything else. Holy shit, she needed to release some tension. He might need to track down Stacy so they could come up with a plan. Send Vati to the spa or get her a man. Something needed to happen before her head exploded.

"Don't get your panties in a twist. Like I was saying before you blew your top again, I can't fix it, the hacker is more experienced than me, but I know someone who might be able to."

He heard her release a breath. "I need better than might. I need can and will."

Jag nodded his head. He knew that. But he wouldn't get her hopes up until he talked to his buddy Colin. "Let me talk to him first, then I'll get back to you. I'm pretty certain he can fix it, but I won't guarantee it."

There were too many beats of silence before his cousin spoke again. He imagined her pacing her office, high heels eating up the carpet, and dark brows furrowed in thought. She was a damned determined woman when it came to J'Adore Dating. It was her brainchild, and a way to keep pace with the changing times and new, innovative ways of dating. Their big boss, Eros, was thrilled with the venture, and a huge supporter of them. That support only went so far though. If things went downhill, or they didn't meet their quota, he could axe everything in a heartbeat, and they would all go back to the bump and run method. It was a pain in the ass, and people nowadays were too wary of strangers randomly running into them.

"Okay," she breathed out easily.

It was a good thing Jag was sitting down. He'd never heard Parvati so calm when it came to the dot com and his

21

inability to fix something. Granted, there were very few things he couldn't fix, but still...it threw him off his game to have her not screaming at the top of her lungs. "Okay," he said warily. "Just okay?"

"Don't push me, Jag. I'm trying to be cool, calm, and collected. When will you have a chance to talk to this person about coming in? Please say it will be soon. As in— right after you get off the phone with me."

Jag dropped his feet to the floor and popped out of his chair. That was the sticking point. He didn't know when he would be able to get hold of Colin. They kept in touch, but he hadn't heard from his friend in at least six months. "Well..." he hedged.

Parvati groaned. "No, please don't tell me there will be a problem with this. I want to hear I'll get hold of him today and he'll be in tonight. Stacy is getting reports that the site hits are increasing, but no one is actually able to do anything. This stupid pop-up keeps appearing and won't let clients navigate around it. I don't want to give people time to cancel memberships and go elsewhere. You know instant gratification is top priority with people these days."

Jag looked out over the IT department. His people had their heads down working, trying to fix the problem. "We're doing all we can to crack it, cuz, but no one has had any luck. I have a couple of my best guys working on rerouting the system so people at least know the site is down. I've told customer service to say we're making improvements for Valentine's Day."

"That's good," she mumbled. "Very good. You know you're going to have to have some kind of change once it comes back up. Do you have a plan already?"

"Uh, no. I was hoping you would come up with something."

Matt, his top IT guy, knocked on his door while peering through the glass window. He motioned with his head that he needed Jag, and Jag was only too happy to get off the phone. Parvati's stress was bleeding through the line no matter how calm she sounded, and he hated that feeling. Avoided it at all times. "Listen, Vati. Matt is knocking on my door and needs me. Think of some cool promotion and let me know. I'll have the guys work on the coding for it so its in place when the website is live again."

"Yeah," she responded. "I'll figure something out." She didn't sound confident, but there wasn't much he could do about that.

"Hey. It'll be okay. I promise. I'll get hold of Colin right after I'm done with Matt. We'll get it fixed and running in no time. This will be a blip on the radar sooner than you know it."

"Thanks, Jag."

Parvati hung up and he felt a little guilty. He knew he should take the hacking seriously, but the pop-up was funny to him. It was probably some nerdy kid pulling a gag meant to annoy and disrupt, not out to cause actual harm.

Scrubbing the back of his neck, he pulled his cell out of his pocket and scrolled through his contacts looking for Colin's number. Matt opened the door and stepped inside. After closing the office blinds, he sidled up close to Jag, peeking over his shoulder.

"Looking for an ex-boyfriend's number," he rumbled softly. Matt's hot breath puffed against Jag's neck, sending a sliver of arousal through him.

Jag's lips curved into a smile. "Nope. I'm good with the boyfriend I have now."

Matt, still looking over Jag's shoulder, slid a hand down Jag's back and cupped his ass at the same time as he nipped his ear. "Good. Your boyfriend is pretty fond of you, too."

"Maybe later he can show me how much he likes me." His own voice came out husky and aroused. Matt never

23

ceased to turn him on, even with the slightest touch.

Matt rocked his hips against Jag's backside. A thrill racing up his spine at the feel of his stiffening erection. Fuck, he loved it when Matt seduced him in the office. "I'm sure that can be arranged." He kissed the side of Jag's neck and stepped away before plopping down in the office chair. He swiveled to face Jag. "Whatcha looking for?"

"You remember Colin Patterson? The guy that came in to talk about hackers and different kinds of hacktivism a while back?"

Matt tugged on Jag's pants, pulling him closer. Slowly and methodically his boyfriend ran his hands up and down Jag's legs, lighting a fire in his cock each time his hands got closer. The man was trying to kill him. They agreed to try not to fool around in the office. They didn't want to get caught by Parvati, or someone who would tell her. Not that they'd stuck to it—yet; but with Parvati in crisis mode, he wasn't sure she wouldn't track him down to make sure he called Colin.

"I remember him. Good-looking guy. About six foot. Glasses. Captivating ice-blue eyes. Wavy chestnut hair long enough to grip with both hands."

Jag rolled his eyes. Matt, of course, would remember those details. They both wondered if Colin would join them for a night of fun, but had never approached him. Something told them he wouldn't, and they weren't ones to pursue the unwilling. "Yeah, that's the guy. Anyway, I think he can help us out. I told Vati I would call him and see."

"Good idea."

Matt nudged Jag's hips until they faced him. His hand went to Jag's zipper, slowly pulling it down. Metal rasping loudly in the silent room the only sound. Jag's cock jerked, sensing the action it was about to get. Knowing Matt was going to take him in hand and, with any luck, mouth. "We agreed," Jag said in token warning. There would never be a time he refused Matt. They had been together for six-months and he was already in love.

Matt snorted. "Have we ever managed to stick to it yet?"

No. He still needed to attempt to be sensible. "What if my cousin walks in?" Even as he said the words, Jag's hands were in Matt's blond hair tugging him closer.

Matt looked up then. Big beautiful, blue eyes full of mischief, sexy ass grin on his face. "Then she'll get an eyeful. Maybe pick up a trick or two."

The thought made him shudder. While Parvati didn't care what he got up to, Jag preferred she didn't see. "Gross. She's my cousin."

Matt shrugged. Jag knew he didn't care if they got caught. In the back of his mind Jag didn't mind either. It would be the easy way to out their relationship. Any other thoughts on the subject fled when Matt reached inside Jag's jeans and pulled out his thickening cock.

"Fuck it," he mumbled when Matt wrapped his lips around the head. Heat spiraled down into his groin. Lighting a fire within. This is what he loved. His boyfriend at his feet sucking his dick like it was the best lollipop in the world. It was made even sweeter knowing they could get caught any minute. That small bit of exhibitionism heightening an already intense moment.

Jag couldn't help but thrust his hips forward, tunneling deeper into Matt's welcoming mouth. Sliding his thick length along Matt's tongue until it tapped the back of his throat. Matt hummed, sending vibrations down his shaft and into his balls. Jag's toes curled in his shoes and eyes rolled into the back of his head. Even as Jag pulled back the tremor followed him, making his hips stutter to a stop.

Matt took advantage of his momentary retreat. Wrapping a hand around Jag's shaft, he made a twisting motion while stroking up and down. Cockhead locked inside his mouth, Matt sucked, licked, and probed it until

Jag moaned out Matt's name. Those jerking motions were small, infinitesimal moves meant to drive Jag crazy and have him racing for a fast finish. Something they both knew needed to happen.

Jag fisted Matt's hair, holding his head steady and thrust in sharp quick movements. A shuffling noise outside his door had him picking up speed and Matt sliding his free hand up Jag's leg. He rolled Jag's balls before tugging them lightly. Jag groaned as the need to come raced down his spine. Shuttling his cock quickly in and out, it didn't take more than a couple of pumps before he let loose the orgasm riding him. "Coming," he muttered seconds before the first spurt hit Matt's tongue.

Matt swallowed him down and sucked him hard. Jag's vision wavered, and he used Matt's head to keep steady. He locked his knees and prayed he could stay up on his feet. Lost in orgasmic bliss, it took a few seconds to realize Matt was suckling his softening flesh and placing kisses along his shaft. A final kiss on the stomach and Matt sat back, smug smile plastered on his handsome face.

Jag tucked his deflated dick away and zipped up his pants. Standing, Matt kissed Jag on the lips, the lingering saltiness of his release still present. It used to weird him out, but ever since he got together with Matt things had been different. It was like sharing a piece of him. A piece of the love they had for each other.

Matt pulled back and walked around him. "Gets better every time."

Jag grinned as someone rapped loudly on the door. "I owe you."

"Just the way I like it," Matt replied, then opened the door. Parvati stood on the other side, forehead scrunched in irritation.

"It smells like sex in here," she said as she stepped inside. She kissed Matt on the cheek, and plopped down in the chair across from Jag's desk. Her arms were crossed over her chest.

26

Jag and Matt stared at each other incredulously. They had kept their relationship private and didn't think she knew. It wasn't that they were ashamed. They only wanted to give it time to develop or bomb out completely.

When no one said anything, she looked between them and burst out laughing. "Oh my, you didn't think I knew? Hilarious. The night watchman caught you two on video and showed it to me. You guys get up to some naughty stuff after hours. I'm cool with it, but, um...try to keep it to a minimum at work please." She shrugged like it wasn't a big deal and started tapping her foot. Anxiety rolled off her in waves. "Enough about that. The number of complaints has risen over the last thirty minutes. I need you to call your fix-it man now. We're in deep trouble, Jag."

CHAPTER THREE

February 2nd – Mid-morning 1045

Colin's phone buzzed grabbing his attention for what felt like the millionth time. He eyed it where it sat on the side table next to him; wishing he could pick it up and at least send out a text for help. His mother made an irritated noise and continued talking. He didn't really know what they were talking about since he'd zoned out minutes after sitting down. He had piles of work at home and a new anti-hacking program to test out.

"I do wish you would turn that thing off, Colin dear. Its rude," she huffed.

"I can't turn it off, mom. I've told you before, I use it for work, and that's probably a client trying to get hold of me." He reached for it and promptly had his hand slapped away. Colin glanced at his mother, and the stern look on her face told him everything he needed to know. He wouldn't be answering his phone any time soon and he'd just turned their short conversation into a nag fest.

If there was one thing Meggie Patterson didn't understand, it was her son's obsession with his work.

Computers were his life. They were how he made his living and what he did in his free time as well. They consumed him and he liked it that way. Computers didn't make demands he couldn't fulfill or get pissed off if he were late.

She just refused to see it and was forever butting into his life. He loved her in spite of it because, well, she was his mom.

At thirty-five, his mother felt it was past time for him to settle down and start producing the next generation of Pattersons. She wanted her house filled with little urchins with sticky fingers and snotty noses. She wanted grandchildren to spoil and make sweet memories with.

If, by some accident of fate, he found a woman who could love a nerdy IT guy with a meddling mother, he would be happy giving her those grandchildren to dote on.

She sighed dramatically, gaining his attention. "Colin, you aren't even listening. We need to discuss the invites for this year's Patterson Paramour Party. Nancy and I have compiled a list of eligible woman and a few select eligible men." She raised her eyebrow in question, and then took a sip of her tea. The long pause meant to be filled by him on whether or not that was a good idea. He wasn't willing to say one-way or the other. If he was going to suffer through this conversation then she needed to as well.

Colin leaned back in his chair suppressing a shudder. The Patterson Marry-My-Son Valentine's Day Party. He should have seen it coming. Would have known it was coming if he'd paid any attention to the date.

"Is it February already?" He knew damn well it was, so why was he trying to drag out the conversation? He needed to tell her he wasn't interested. He would never find a love match at the parties she threw with her best friend. Colin was beginning to see the beauty in his Dad's obsession with model trains.

"It's the second. We've already lost one day." She set

her teacup down and picked up a notebook he hadn't noticed earlier. "Nancy thinks the Baker twins are both single again, and Janet got divorced over the summer. Oh, I liked Janet, such a nice girl. I was sad to hear her husband cheated on her. I did wonder about them though. He had a bit of a wandering eye, if you know what I mean. The better for you though; so we'll definitely add her. You can catch her on the rebound."

Colin's eyebrows shot up to his hairline in surprise. "Rebound?" He didn't think he was that terrible that he needed to catch a woman while she was in mid-devastation.

"Yes dear, while she's feeling a bit down about men. You can sweep in and make nice, charm her off her feet. I don't think she'd mind being married to a computer guy. You two would make such beautiful children together," she said wistfully.

Shit, she's serious this year. Usually he mother just invited a couple of her friends and their families, hoping they would bring their single female relatives. "What about the Baker twins?" Why couldn't he keep his mouth shut?

His mom's head popped up from her list. "Cindy or Lauren? I always thought Lauren was the prettier of the two, but she can be such a snot at times. She thinks she's better than everyone else. A pretentious one, that girl."

"Um…" Colin didn't even know what to say to that. He thought they were both snobs and wasn't attracted to either. They picked on him when he was a scrawny little boy, and it didn't change in high school when he was a taller, yet nerdy, scrawny boy.

"Cindy is so sweet though. If I had to pick, I would go with Cindy. Maybe she's a wild little thing in the sack."

Luckily for Colin, his phone rang again. He snatched the phone up and noticed the caller. "I'm sorry mom, I really have to take this. Do whatever you'd like. You know best. I'll give you a call later to check in."

Before his mom could protest, he swooped in and kissed her on the cheek. He was out the door seconds later. Without looking like the hounds of hell were on his feet, he rushed to his car and got in. The car hooked up with the Bluetooth in his phone, and he answered as he sedately reversed down his mom's driveway.

"Jag, man, how are you doing?"

"Colin?" Jag sounded surprised, which was funny since he was the one who called.

"You did mean to call me, right? You know, it actually doesn't matter. You just got me out of a painful conversation with my mom. What's up?"

Jag's light-hearted laugh streamed through the phone, brightening Colin's mood. It had been a while since he last talked to his friend. Longer than it should have been, but he'd been busy and he was sure Jag had been too.

"Glad to help. Maybe you can do me a solid then. I've got a problem down here at J'Adore and wondered if you might have time to check it out. I think its right up your alley."

Colin was intrigued. J'Adore had a large clientele and elaborate computer networking system and program. When he had gone there to do a class on hackers, he'd practically drooled over the equipment Jag worked with. No expense was spared in the running of the dating company.

He checked the time on his watch. He had a meeting at one that could last a couple of hours. "I'm kind of tied up until late this afternoon. I wouldn't be able to get there until probably after you close up shop."

"That's fine. We've been hacked and my cousin is having kittens over it. As long as you can get here today, it would be great. Maybe her head won't explode and my aunt won't kill me."

Colin wondered about the woman in charge at

31

J'Adore. He hadn't met her on his last visit, but heard from almost everyone he ran into that she was a hard taskmaster with a romantic heart. She was in love with love and thought everyone should get the chance to experience it.

"Colin? You still there?" Jag's voice came through the speakers of the car jolting him from his thoughts.

"Yeah. Um, if you don't mind me coming so late, I can come by. How about around six? That will give me time to finish up my meeting, grab some food, and change out of this suit."

"One of those meetings. I don't envy you. Vati had to threaten me with a visit from my aunt to get me to wear a suit for one of our cousin's weddings."

Colin heard another man's voice rumble in the background.

"Hey, I have to go. Parvati is looking for me again. At least now I'll have something good to tell her. Check in at the reception desk when you get here. Same place you went when you were here before. I'll leave your name so they know to expect you."

"Sounds good. See you later." Colin hung up and the music kicked in. He tapped along with the tune on the steering wheel and grinned, excitement coursing through his blood. A new project that had his name written all over it, maybe one that would last long enough to get out of going to his mom's Valentine's party. A desperate guy could only hope.

CHAPTER FOUR

February 2nd – Late Afternoon 615pm

Parvati stood at the reception desk tapping her fingers on the counter. This guy, Colin, was fifteen minutes late, and she was losing patience…fast. The entire day she had fielded phone calls from angry clients and rushed back and forth between her office and Jag's, bothering him with questions and status updates.

It irritated the hell out of him and, at one point; he kicked her out of the building and told her to take a chill pill. He actually physically escorted her outside the building, went back inside, and locked her out. He waved at her from the other side of the glass door until she stormed away.

She should fire his ass, but knew she wouldn't. Her mom would kill her for firing him. At least the jerk was nice enough to give her a couple of dollars for tea. It was the only thing she could think to do that would waste time and give her a chance to figure out a way back inside.

Revenge would come later and, most likely, in the form of horrific and embarrassing stories told to his boyfriend. She couldn't wait.

Thoughts of Jag's love life had her moving around the desk to sit in the receptionist's chair. She was thrilled for him and jealous as all get out. She'd noticed the looks of affection going on between the two men over the last few months and wondered, not for the first time, why they didn't tell her. Did they think she would be angry or force one of them to quit? Did they think she would frown upon their relationship and not support them? Jag loved Matt and that was good enough for her. She only ever wanted him to be happy.

Parvati knew love happened when least expected and that a person had no control over it. When love came calling, she felt a person should embrace it. Nurture it and show it the respect it deserved. You should shout it from the rooftops and let the whole world know. Just because she couldn't find it, didn't mean she wouldn't celebrate when others did.

The double glass doors opened as her thoughts strayed down a path she didn't want to go. Her love life — or better yet — non-existent love life.

A man came strolling in, blinking rapidly behind dark-rimmed square glasses. The bright lights of the building in stark contrast to the oppressing gloom outside. She studied him as he crossed the floor and wondered if he was the running late IT savant Colin.

He wore an open dark gray casual coat over a deep blue T-shirt. Well-worn jeans hugged his lean hips and thighs. A pair of dark blue Converse was on his feet. He walked with a confidence and ease she hadn't seen in far too long. It was sexy as hell and completely unexpected.

All of the guys she knew or dated showed up in expensive suits and wore their overblown egos as if all those around should bow down to them. Maybe that's why it never works, she marveled. She loved a man with a brain and got stuck on the idea of dating engineers and lawyers. Could it really be time to change that? She chewed on her lip as she thought it through.

"Excuse me, miss?" He leaned down to catch her eye.

Parvati shook her head. "Oh! I'm so sorry."

He smiled, his eyes crinkling at the corners with laughter. "Don't worry about it. I'm guessing you've been waiting for me to show up. I'm Colin Patterson. Sorry to keep you here after hours. Hopefully, your boss doesn't get too mad. I heard she's a slave-driver." He chuckled and shoved his hands into his jeans pockets.

Parvati stood and opened her mouth to tell him it was fine, but promptly shut it when she realized what he said. "Slave driver?" Is that what people thought of her?

"Yeah, Jag told me she was driving him and the staff nuts because of what happened. That she's been a tyrant all day."

"Tyrant?" She whispered, surprised to hear her cousin talk about her like that. She knew she was uptight when it came to the company, especially today. She didn't realize she drove him and everyone else nuts, or that they thought she was a tyrant. Was it that bad working for her?

He cringed when she repeated the word. "Sorry, I guess I shouldn't talk about her like that. She is your boss after all. If you could just point me in the direction of her office, I'll head to it and you can take off. I'm sure a pretty girl like you has something better to do than sit around here waiting on some IT guy."

Parvati blinked a couple of times trying to get her head in the game. Usually she would be ripping this guy a new one but she wasn't. She didn't know if it had to do with the fact she needed him or that she was in stunned shock about knowing people talked about her behind her back. Thinking people liked you and having that bubble burst would fuck anyone up.

"If you'll follow me," she murmured and blindly made her way to her office. Silently they rode the elevator up two flights. As she stepped out on her floor, the words slave driver and tyrant chased her down the hall.

*****

Colin followed the pretty receptionist down the hall to her boss's office. He passed by a break room, bathrooms, another bank of elevators, and weaved through what looked to be an open office space with tons of cubicles, barely taking note of any of it. The woman in front of him garnered all of his attention. A parade of circus elephants could have tromped by, and he wouldn't have noticed them.

The undulation of her hips and lushness of her ass beneath her skirt intrigued him. Her tiny waist begged for his hands to wrap around it. Her wavy, deep brown— almost black—hair swayed as she walked. His hands itched to run up and down the bare skin of her arms.

She was sexy in a way he never imagined. Feminine but with an air of tightly reigned in self-control. God, he wanted to ask her to stick around while he dealt with her boss's problem. Take her out for a drink and loosen her up. Listen to her say his name; hell, just get her to talk.

He didn't know what made him spew from the mouth when he walked up to the reception desk. He saw her sitting there lost in thought. Her beautiful deep brown eyes were glazed, and the cutest little frown creased her forehead. Whatever bothered the woman, he had the overriding urge to soothe her. So he talked and tried to get her to smile or laugh. It hadn't worked. If anything, her frown deepened and the color leeched from her tan face.

Bagging on the boss probably wasn't his best approach to someone that worked for her. From her reaction, her loyalty appeared to run deep. For all he knew, they could be related or something equally horrifying. He didn't mean anything bad by it. He just wanted to break the ice. Now it was too late to backtrack and right his wrongs.

They turned left at a bank of glassed-in, cookie-cutter offices and arrived in an open reception area. A desk sat to

36

the left, chairs to the right, both devoid of activity. Looked like the secretary hadn't bothered to stay. Lucky for him or her.

The woman, whose name he needed to get before she left, passed the desk and went straight into the office. She flipped on the light and motioned to the plush chairs in front of the large oak desk. He took the one on the right, easing down into the soft, chocolate brown leather. He suppressed the sigh that wanted to escape. Not only did the company have the best equipment but also the most comfortable, expensive furniture he'd had the pleasure of sitting in.

"I'm surprised your boss isn't in here waiting. Jag said her head was close to exploding this morning. The way he described her, I expected she would be waiting, talons out and breathing fire," he chuckled uncomfortably. There he went with his mouth again, shoving his foot in with no problem. Why couldn't he shut the hell up?

"Yes. I'm sure it would seem that way to him," she murmured from somewhere behind him. "If you'll give me a moment, I'll get everyone here."

Twisting in his seat, he watched as she left the room and went to the secretary's desk. Maybe she was the woman who sat there. He could only hope she stayed until after the meeting with the owner.

The woman picked up the phone, turned her back to him, and made a call. Dropping the receiver back in place, she leaned against the front of the desk, arms crossed over her chest, tight skirt hugging her backside.

Minutes went by and she sat unmoving. Deep voices could be heard coming down the hall, and Colin hoped it would be the owner, Parvati, and his friend Jag. Instead, two men walked into the room; Jag and a good-looking blond man Colin remembered from his one other time there.

"Go on in," he heard her say coolly.

When Jag and the other man came in, Colin stood with his hand outstretched. "How're you doing, Jag?"

Jag shook his hand and motioned to the man next to him. "This is Matt, not sure if you remember him."

Colin grinned upon hearing the name. "Oh yeah. You're Jag's top guy. Nice to see you again."

Matt and Jag snorted.

"Have a seat gentlemen." The receptionist pushed a chair in, placing it behind Jag. They all sat and Colin was about to ask about Jag's cousin when the woman walked around the desk and sat down as if she belonged there.

Spine rigid, she laced her fingers together on the desktop, and an angry gleam shown through her eyes.

"Oh shit!" Three pairs of eyes focused on him. Two questioning his outburst and one shooting daggers. All this time he had been talking to the owner of J'Adore Dating, Parvati Amata. Talking about how much of a ballbuster she was, how crazy she made people. Telling her people thought she was a fire-breathing dragon hell bent on destruction.

Okay, so maybe not that specifically, but he didn't doubt that was how she took it. This was not good.

CHAPTER FIVE

February 2nd – Late Afternoon 6:35pm

Parvati closed her eyes, shutting out the handsome yet shocked face of Colin. She breathed in deeply and slowly counted down from ten. It was the only thing she could do to rein in her anger.

10…

9…

8…

"Vati?" Jag asked cautiously.

She held up her hand, cutting him off. She was, stupidly, hurt by the things Colin had said about her. She didn't know him and he didn't know her. That he heard those things from Jag, or that Jag gave him that impression of her, made it almost unbearable. If there was one person she thought had her back, it was her cousin.

7…

6…

5…it isn't his fault. You need his help. Calm down and do your best not to kill him.

4…

3…

2…

1…by the time she reached the end, she felt ready to talk. Opening her eyes, she mentally shut down every emotion welling up inside her and studied the three men in front of her. Concern vibrated from Jag and Matt. Colin appeared embarrassed. None of them would get a reaction from her. This was about the business, and that always came first.

"I appreciate you coming in after hours, Mr. Patterson. My cousin Jagjit said you were brilliant when it came to hackers and breaking through what they do. Since he and his team haven't been able to crack it, I have the utmost confidence you'll be able to. I've looked up your accolades and accomplishments online, and I have to say I'm very impressed." She had to work to keep her tone of voice strong yet neutral, when all she wanted to do was rage and kick them all out. They thought she was a rage-filled, ball-busting bitch, well, they were in for a surprise. She would be calm and accommodating, even if it killed her. She also wouldn't be staying around to make sure Colin had everything he needed as she'd originally planned.

Who cared if she'd told those snakes, Jag and Matt, they could head home after Colin got there. Fuck them! This was their area of expertise, and they would now have the pleasure of sticking around in case they were needed.

Colin opened his mouth, but no words came out. He looked to her cousin, then back at her. He tipped his head down quickly in affirmation. "Thank you," he rumbled roughly. The deep timber of his voice skated down her spine seductively, and she hated the feeling. Hated that it turned her on with those two simple words. If only he hadn't been an ass earlier.

She couldn't stay in the room anymore. Rising, she shoved her chair out of the way before grabbing her tailored jacket off the back. The men stood as well. As she slipped the coat on, she looked squarely at her cousin as she buttoned it up. "I'm sure Colin will appreciate you staying in case he needs help. You'll be able to brief him on what happened better than me."

Pulling her purse from the bottom drawer of the desk, she hitched it up on her shoulder. Rounding the desk, she held her hand out to Colin. Swallowing hard, she willed her hand to stay steady. "Thank you for coming in. Jagjit and Matt know how to get hold of me if you have any questions they can't answer. I don't expect that to be an issue."

Colin slid his larger hand into hers, sparking a jolt of electricity. He looked into her face with a searching gaze. His eyebrows furrowed, and she could see he wanted to say something. Too damn bad for him. She didn't want to hear it.

Tugging her hand, he let it go, and she instantly missed the feel of it in hers. Suck it up, Vati. She strode to the door on wobbly legs, but was stopped by her cousin's voice.

"Stop right there, dearest cousin. I need a word." His toned brooked no argument. "Matt, can you show Colin to my office? He can work from there."

"Sure," Matt said, concern softening his voice.

There was rustling behind her, probably them getting up, maybe Jag hugging his boyfriend and kissing him quickly. There were murmured voices and a shifting of bodies. She shut them out and concentrated on her breathing. Wouldn't her therapist love to know the technique actually worked? Crafty bitch. Now, Parvati was going to have to thank the annoying woman. She wanted to smile at the thought, but refused to in case the men were watching her. Soft treading on the carpet had her stepping to the side.

Matt passed and looked at her quickly. Not once, since she had known him, had she been rude to him. She was always happy to see him; thrilled Jag had someone so special in his life. Something she, herself, had yet to achieve.

Colin stepped up beside her and rested his hand on her arm. The heat of his fingers scorched her and left her craving the feel of them all over her body. The reaction surprised her and was out of the norm. She'd just met him, and he'd talked shit about her. Maybe what they said was right; you always fall for the ones who treat you the worst.

"I'm sorry, Parvati. If I had known…"

Her angry gaze snapped to his troubled one. "If you'd known, you would have what? Waited until I was gone and you could gossip with Jag behind my back? Would you have had a good laugh at my expense too?" She hated the hurt bleeding through. Why she felt that way was beyond her. It had to be because her day had been complete shit, and everything that transpired between them was the icing on the horrible cake that was her life.

Colin sighed and looked at her with regret in his eyes. "No," he started to say, but she cut him off again.

"Don't worry about it, Colin. It isn't your fault. At least now I know what people think about me."

He looked as if he was going to say more. "Please, don't. I've had enough for today," she said, and didn't bother keeping the pleading tone out of her voice. She was so close to cracking, and she didn't want to do it in front of him. Her jagged pride knew it would be a mistake. She would regret it if she let him see her broken down.

He nodded and left the room. Jag closed the door softly, and then stood in front of her, arms crossed over his chest.

"What was that about? I thought you were going to stay with him tonight."

She scoffed. "No. I changed my mind once I heard all of the things you said about me."

"What I said about you?" Confusion colored his words and painted across his face. Of course, he wouldn't know.

"I'm a slave-driver, who makes those around me nuts while I'm being a talon-bearing, fire-breathing tyrant."

Jag's eyes widened in surprise.

"Yeah, that's what Colin told me when he apparently thought I was the lowly receptionist kept here by her horrible boss."

"I didn't know," Jag exclaimed.

"I don't know why not. He heard all of those words from you. Jesus, Jag, I thought you were on my side, and I don't know what hurts worse; knowing my cousin talks about me behind my back and my entire staff thinks I'm this horrible person, or that a man I am ridiculously attracted to already hates me." Shit, she didn't expect that last part to come tumbling out. Her shoulders slumped in exhaustion. All Parvati wanted to do was go home and throw on her pajamas and watch reality TV. She should have stayed in bed this morning. Maybe if she had none of this would have happened.

She reached for the doorknob when Jag went to gather her up in his arms. She didn't want his comfort. Quickly, she stepped back out of his reach. "No. I can't do this right now. I've had the worst day possible and hearing all of that," she waved her hand at the door the guys disappeared through, "I'm too hurt right now. I still can't believe you talk about me behind my back. I need to go home and put this day to rest. I can't bear to spend hours on end with a man who thinks all of that about me. Not without having the time to build my defenses. This is where you're going to have to step up to the plate, Jag. I'm done."

Parvati didn't wait for her cousin to say anything. She yanked open the door, and was surprised to see Matt and

43

Colin sitting in the reception area. Their heads swiveled in her direction. Had they heard her sad confession? A rush of heat gathered at the backs of her eyes, tears threatening to fall. She would not do that here. Nodding curtly, she left without making an even bigger fool of herself.

CHAPTER SIX

February 2nd – Going on Midnight

Colin slumped in his borrowed chair and tipped his head back. As soon as his head settled, his eyes slammed shut. He massaged the bridge of his nose with his thumb and forefinger in an attempt to ease the pain trying to form.

Fuck, he was tired.

The morning visit with his mother, the afternoon meeting with potential investors, and then his royal fuck up with the very delectable Parvati—all of which made for a long, shitty day. He didn't need to fix anything with his mom or the investors, but damn if he didn't need to do some damage control with Parvati. Not because he was working for her and, in essence, insulted his temporary employer. Not really.

No, he needed to fix things because he had a driving need to get close to her, and that wouldn't happen if she spent the rest of the time he was there pissed off at him.

He had convinced Matt to wait for Jag, and for a

chance to apologize, yet again, to Parvati. He still didn't know why his dumb mouth didn't stay shut around her.

Shit. Yeah he did. He wanted to take her worries away and get her to smile at him. He bet it would light up her face; make those brown eyes of hers sparkle and those full, pink lips curve upward teasing him.

But when she walked out on the verge of tears, he didn't have the balls to chase her down and make her relive what he'd said. He wasn't that thickheaded. He did need to figure out a way to take back everything without causing further damage.

Jesus, just saying her name in his head and envisioning her made him hard. He thought she was beautiful sitting there at the reception desk, but when he got a good look at her, found out who she was — he realized she was so much more. A beautiful, intelligent woman running a fast-growing company was a major turn-on in his book.

Jag also didn't waste any time backtracking everything he said about her. He made damn sure Colin knew his cousin wasn't really the fire-breathing dragon he'd made her out to be. Jag freely admitted he liked to pick on her, but that she had a heart of gold. She had even offered to stay with Colin so Jag and Matt could go out on a date. That was before both of them made a mess of everything. Jag swore it wasn't Colin's fault but he knew better. The little voice in the back of his head that kept telling him to shut-up had been trying to do him a favor.

In the end, they'd both fucked up, and Colin was sure it would be harder for him to get Parvati's forgiveness than it would be Jag's. It was completely insane too since he'd just met her. Normally he wouldn't be bothered if she didn't like him, if he'd pissed her off. He was at J'Adore to do a job, not get a girlfriend. This time, for some inexplicable reason, it mattered. He wanted her.

"You should go home and get some sleep." Jag's voice yanked him from his thoughts.

46

"You're right, I should." Too bad he couldn't get up out of the chair to follow through. Exhaustion settled in his bones, making it impossible.

Jag flopped into the chair across from him and kicked his feet up on the desk. "How's it going?"

Colin shrugged. "It could be better, but it's getting there. I think I can have you back up and running by Friday at the earliest."

Jag's sigh held a note of frustration. "Vati isn't going to be too happy about that."

"I'm sorry. I wish it could be sooner." If it were, maybe then he'd impress her enough to make up for his dickhead behavior.

"Not your fault. We've found holes in our protocols that lead to this problem. I just hope we stopped it in time to prevent more clients from seeing we're screwed up."

"You guys got the site offline and put up the dummy page, that should have helped. I think I've found the source, but need some more time sorting the code he's put in to prevent it from being deleted. Thankfully, you have a good amount of backup data we can recover from if need be. You'll lose anything new from within the last month, but it's better than nothing. Once we have this all sorted out, I think you need to look at your backup process and some better protection software."

"Thanks. I expect you'll have some suggestions on that."

"I do. Some of it's my own work not yet on the market. I'm happy to share them with you."

Jag snorted. "For how much? You're stuff is the best and, though I'm not saying we can't afford it, I don't want to piss off my cousin any more."

For free if she'll forgive me. But he didn't say that. "I'm sure we can work something out."

Jag studied him for a moment, making Colin slightly uncomfortable. He shifted in his chair while waiting for Jag to say whatever was on his mind. It didn't take long, thankfully. "How would you feel about being on retainer here?"

He hesitated to answer. A small part of him liked the idea of being part of something that involved Parvati. He could wear her down over time, and possibly get her to agree to a date. Show her he wasn't some guy with the social ineptitude of a rock. Wishful thinking on his part. "Once you guys are up and running, I doubt there's anything else I can help you with."

"As much as I'd like to think that, I don't want to chance it. I thought you could come in once a month and help us go through the system. Make sure everything is up to snuff. It wouldn't take much of your time, and I'm sure it would ease my cousin's mind. She was really impressed with everything you've done. I know she looked forward to meeting you tonight. I'm sorry it didn't go better."

Colin couldn't stop from cringing. He was happy to hear she liked his work but, at the same time, it made him feel like an ass again. He hadn't bothered learning anything about her, and now it was too late for a great first impression. "Listen, about earlier. I didn't know it was her I was talking to. And that's not an excuse for my behavior. I never should have said any of it. I was just trying to get her to smile."

Jag grinned knowingly. "And in the process of hitting on her you insulted her. Shit happens. She'll get over it."

Colin wasn't so sure. There was a spark between them. He'd felt it when he slid his hand against hers. Her soft, delicate fingers wrapping around his felt good, so good; in fact, he didn't want to let go. "I wasn't technically hitting on her. She looked so worried, and I wanted to lighten the mood. I should have guessed though. I don't know why I didn't see it at the time; you two look a lot alike."

"Our moms were twins so I can see what you're

saying. Vati and I grew up together, and we're more like brother and sister. They treat us like it too. I don't believe you would have known who she was by guessing. A lot of our family works here. She could have been any one of my female cousins. You didn't meet Vati when you were here the first time around so you couldn't have known. Seriously, don't worry about it. She'll be back to her usual uptight self in the morning. Speaking of which," he glanced at his watch and winced, "I told Matt we would go home a while ago. He's probably waiting for me in the car."

Jag stood and waited for Colin. The program he was running would take the rest of the evening. There was no reason for him to stick around. Plus, he needed some sleep in order to be at his best when he groveled and begged for forgiveness. He may not know why it mattered, but he would go with his gut feeling. The one that said he desperately needed Parvati to not hate him, that she was important.

They walked out of the room and Colin followed along as Jag locked up.

"You have a thing for her, don't you?"

The question surprised Colin, who was lost in his thoughts per usual. "Uh, yeah. I guess. She's pretty — beautiful actually. It isn't just that though. From the things you told me, I'd say she was a dedicated woman with a romantic side. So deeply romantic that she aspires to help all people experience finding their love for all eternity. She sounds like someone I wouldn't mind getting to know better."

Jag grunted. "That's Vati. She loves love, but love doesn't seem to love her. She has the worst luck with men." They stopped at the bank of elevators, and Jag pushed the down button before facing Colin.

Colin wasn't too sure where Jag was trying to go with the conversation. "Are you trying to warn me off or just give me a heads up?"

Jag shrugged. One of those one shouldered things that didn't mean anything. "Just letting you know. Do with it what you want, but I think she could actually fall for you. It was a crazy day and normally she wouldn't have put up with someone talking to her like that. She's an in your face kind of person. The fact that you got away with it makes me wonder if there might be more than her wanting to jump your bones."

She wants to jump my bones? "How do you know that?" He could get on board with it if that were true. The elevator pinged and they stepped in. He didn't wait for Jag to answer. It really didn't matter. "What do you suggest I do?" Colin would take some advice from the man close enough to be considered a brother. He hadn't been instantly attracted to a woman in so long; he was beginning to wonder if the world was against him. Yeah, he encountered plenty of attractive women, but none who made him want to press her up against a wall and ravish her. None who made him want to chase her gloom away and cuddle until she felt better. Just cuddle, nothing else.

"If you're serious about her, then go for it. If you're looking for some fun and intend on breaking her heart— back the fuck away. I may pick on and tease my cousin, but I won't stand by and see her get hurt. She's been through that enough."

Colin nodded and they rode the elevator down in silence. He had a lot to think through. He glanced at his watch, less than eight hours to figure out if he wanted more than a casual romp with the lovely Parvati Amara. His beautiful Indian princess with a brain for business and a heart full of love waiting to be tapped.

CHAPTER SEVEN

February 3rd – Too early for some people 6am

Parvati climbed into the elevator, hit the button for the third floor, and leaned back on the railing. It was too damn early to be at work again, but she wanted to get some things done before the rest of the staff came in. She needed the peace and quiet before the stresses of the day piled up and turned her hair gray.

Taking a sip of her hot tea, she sighed in delight. Right before leaving the house, she steeped her favorite chamomile tea, honey vanilla with a hint of orange, in her ceramic to-go tea mug in the hope it would lend itself to keeping her calm and lessen the anxious tension she could feel slowly building within. So far, it was doing an outstanding job. The nutty vanilla and slight orange twist wound its way through her, easing nerves still frayed from the day before. The real test would be when the day officially started and she found out if the site was anywhere close to being fixed.

Jag didn't get hold of her during the evening, so she assumed things weren't put to rights. Or, he knew how pissed off she was and avoided her completely. With her luck, it was a combination of the two. The site wasn't fixed, and he knew she would blow a gasket. The clever guy knew better than to bother her with news like that.

The elevator dinged then stopped. Stepping out onto her floor, the automatic lights came on and lit the way to her office. The place was quiet. No low hum of computers warming up. No chatter coming from the break room as people got their morning cups of coffee or tea.

Being a tea drinker, she made sure it was well stocked with all of her favorites from subtle white teas to seasonal Rooibos, along with an array of honeys, rock sugar, and creamers. The coffee drinkers weren't neglected, but she catered to what she liked. Just one of the perks of being the boss.

Striding into her office, she deposited her mug and purse on the desk, booted up her computer and took off her black coat. As she sat down in her chair, she couldn't help but reflect on the previous day. It had been shitty. One of the worst ones to date. She let the hacker break her mentally, and she never should have allowed that happen. Not to mention, she neglected her morning ritual. Her prayers played a huge role in her life and one day without them was one too many.

"It's a new day. It will be better," she breathed out. Closing her eyes, she took a calming breath, opening her mind, and sent a prayer to her namesake.

Sarvu Mangala Maangalye, Shive Sarvaartha Saadhike

Sharanye Tryambake Gaurii, Naaraaynii Namostute

Goddess Parvati is the auspiciousness of all that is auspicious.

She is the consort of the Lord Shiva, who grants every

desire of one's heart.

I adore such Devi Parvati, who loves all her children.

I bow to the great mother, who has given refuge to me.

The link between her mind and that of the Goddess Parvati crackled and sparked. Heat twisted and turned around her body, the invisible wave caressing her eagerly. Feather light wisps of sensation smoothed across her brow, down the bridge of her nose, and over her lips. Her scalp tingled as her hair lifted. Her breath stopped up in her chest as a soft voice drifted over her ears. "You will have as you desire."

Parvati's eyes popped open and she looked around the room. There was no one there. Logically, she knew that. The scent of saffron clung heavy to the air. A bittersweet, earthy softness, which couldn't be mistaken for anything else. It reminded her of home and family. But most of all, it was the scent of her namesake.

Excitement coursed through her upon realization that she may finally get her wish. The only uncertainty was if that wish was for the site to get back up and running, or if she would finally find the man of her dreams.

Feeling better than she had in weeks, she dropped her purse into a drawer, sipped her tea, and dug into the work she'd ignored the day before. There was a lot that could be done not involving the site and its problems. Emails needed to go out. There was a meeting with her financial officer. Also on her agenda, a phone conference with a counterpart in the United Kingdom. She knew in her heart that this day would be better than the previous.

Three hours and copious amounts of work later, Stacy knocked on her door.

"Come in," Parvati called out, and hit send on the email she'd been working on. When she looked up, Stacy stood in the doorway. She cast a nervous glance behind her, and then looked at Parvati.

Whatever Stacy had to say, Parvati refused to get upset. Her Goddess had spoken to her. The first time in over five years that it had happened. The last time was when Parvati came up with the idea for J'Adore Dating.

J'Adore wasn't like most run of the mill dating websites. It catered to the Mystics of the world. The paranormal beings and lesser Gods and Goddesses, like her, that roamed the earth. She found matches for them whether human, crossbreed, or pure supernatural. She didn't discriminate.

"What's up, Stacy?" Parvati asked, lacing her fingers together.

"Jag is here, and there's a hot to trot geek with him." She wiggled her eyebrows lasciviously and grinned.

Parvati's eyebrow rose at the remark. She didn't think Colin screamed geek. Just the opposite, in fact. He was sex on a stick, and his damn glasses made her panties melt. "And how do you know he's a geek?"

"He's got that same I'm-too-smart-for-you vibe going on, just like Jag," she whispered theatrically. She cast a glance behind her quickly again. "There's something about him that makes me nervous. I can't quite place my finger on it."

Parvati laughed at Stacy's behavior. She knew it irritated the woman when men thought she was just a pretty face. If they knew she could read ancient text, call upon fire to do her bidding in human form, or shift into a dragon; she doubted they'd treat her that way. And what was with her nervous feeling? Stacy could hold her own against a human, which Colin certainly was. There was nothing threatening about him. He came with good references and a recommendation from her cousin. That was all she needed to know.

"Have them come in," she said. She took a fortifying sip of her tea as she waited for the men. Stacy ducked out the door and closed it as soon as their asses cleared the space.

Both men wore solemn, apologetic looks on their faces. Parvati had to keep from chuckling. Both were so serious but, as far as she was concerned, nothing would faze her today.

"Have a seat. Did either of you want something to drink?" Her finger hovered over the call button to get hold of Stacy just in case.

They shook their heads in unison and folded their large bodies into the leather seats in front of her desk. She waited for them to get comfortable. "How did it go last night? Did you make any progress?"

"I'm sorry, Vati, about yesterday," Jag said, ignoring her question. "You know how I like to joke around with you. I took it too far. Colin didn't know it was you, and he would never say anything like that maliciously."

Parvati tilted her head to the side and studied her cousin. There were prominent dark circles under his eyes and considering he was Indian that was saying a lot. His black hair stood in various directions disheveled, like he kept running his fingers through it. His jaw clenched and he appeared contrite. He looked tired and must not have slept much the night before.

She let her gaze wander over to Colin. His intense ice blue eyes bored into her, and his forehead was crinkled. He, too, clenched his jaw and appeared unsettled. "You looked as if the weight of the world was on your shoulders and, knowing what I do now, I would say that's pretty accurate. I wanted to make you smile by joking around about the boss. Break the ice. Everyone jokes about the guy in charge. It's not an excuse for my behavior, and it shouldn't have happened. It was a long day and you were sitting there lost in a daze." He leaned forward in his chair, resting his forearms on his knees. "Shit. I don't know what I was thinking."

She didn't know either and, at this point, didn't care.

She was captivated by him. The deep timber of his voice. The strength she could see rippling through his arms. He wore a T-shirt that gripped his biceps, straining to keep them contained. The muscles in his arms flexed as he talked with his hands. And, oh my, what big hands he had. *The better to caress my body with.*

She licked her lips and admired him more, letting her gaze trail back up until she looked into his face. His crystal clear eyes got her every time. She could get lost staring into them all day. His glasses emphasizing them, making them stand out against his dark hair and pale skin. Their gazes locked and held steady. The desire she saw within his had her pulse picking up. Arousal threaded through her and peaked her nipples behind the soft lace of her bra. The silk shirt she had on would do nothing to hide her reaction to him. And she wasn't sure she wanted to hide at all.

Jag cleared his throat, and she blinked rapidly. Colin sat back in his chair, question written all over his face. He looked confused about her reaction to him. She probably would be too if she were in his shoes.

Parvati turned her focus to her computer screen, clicking on random windows she had up. She needed something else to look at. Something to distract her from the man sitting across from her. "Don't worry about it, either of you. Yesterday is done and over with. I've moved on. I'm more concerned about the progress in fixing the hack, and if there is a way to track back to whomever did it. I'm thinking about pressing charges for malicious mischief or computer trespass. Whoever this guy is, he's out to harm the company. If we don't stop him, he'll do it to someone else when he feels they've crossed him in some manner."

"Okay," Jag dragged out. "Colin said he hoped to have us up and running by Friday. I know you like having two weeks before Valentine's Day to promote the site, but we'll have to get it all in the week before."

Parvati contemplated the timeline. She could make it

work. She could postpone the television ad and revamp it to include a deep discount on signing up. The ads across various websites would stay the same. They were set up so far in advance, she didn't want to make adjustments and give her spots away. The J'Adore Annual Party was already set up and invitations sent out so there would be no change there. They just wouldn't be able to include as many new sign ups as past years.

She could use the next couple of days to work with her financial officer to go over the numbers and glance over the taxes. Start on some of the more mundane things she was involved in.

She nodded her head, pleased with her plans. "Friday is good. I wish it were sooner, but I know you guys will do the best you can." Rising from her seat, she stuck her hand out to Colin. "I'm sorry about yesterday as well. I should have introduced myself right away. I am truly glad to have you here helping out. Please make sure you bill us for your hours, even if it's at an overtime rate. Getting the company back up and running is my top priority."

Colin stood and slid his palm against hers. At that moment, she wished she hadn't gotten to her feet. Her knees wobbled as the heat from his hand spread down her arm and through her chest. The warmth fanned out and flowed down into her core. "Oh my," she breathed out softly.

This man affected her on a primal level. Something she had yet to experience with any other person. He could be dangerous to her romantic heart—if she allowed it. For all she knew, he had some cutie waiting for him at home every night. Someone to lie in bed with as he tapped away on his computer and she read a book or watched TV. Someone to cuddle up next to on cold nights.

*****

Colin locked is legs, stopping them from buckling as electricity shot through him. It was the second time that had happened with this woman. He wasn't sure if it was

57

because of his attraction to her, or because he was so damn relieved she'd forgiven him.

Surprise didn't even cover how he felt when she apologized for the evening before. She didn't need to as far as he was concerned. He was the one that ran off at the mouth. If he had been paying more attention, hadn't been exhausted from his day, he would have seen how deeply his words affected her and how much she resembled Jag.

Her soft exclamation broke through his thoughts, and he looked down to see he still had hold of her hand. He cleared his throat. "I'll do my best to get you back up before Friday. I know how much this business means to you. And again—I'm sorry."

She smiled softly and his heart flipped. "Thank you."

Their gazes caught and he felt himself lean into her. The damn desk was in the way, though.

"I'll just head down to my office," Jag interrupted. Colin dropped her hand and took a step back. He bumped into the chair, stumbled slightly, and grimaced. He was making a fool out of himself. *Nerd boy strikes again.*

"Sorry. I should head down with him," he mumbled and felt heat lick across his face. When would he ever make a good impression on this woman? Stepping wide of the damn chair, he followed Jag to the door.

Parvati's light laugh reached across the room and grabbed him by the balls. She sounded happy and carefree. He liked her like that. Though maybe not at his expense. "If you need anything let me know," she said. He didn't miss the emphasis on the word *anything.* Would she be open to a kiss from him? Maybe go out on a date with him?

Colin looked over his shoulder at her and saw her eyes rise from where she'd been looking. Doing some quick calculations, he figured out what she'd been doing. *She's checking me out.* He grinned and when he got to the door, he closed it and locked it. Backtracking, he strode across

58

the room until he was next to her. She turned toward him, her mouth open in surprise. Her breathing picked up, and the pulse at the base of her neck beat wildly.

Without putting any thought into what he was about to do, he placed his hands on the sides of her face and kissed her. A slow, sensual assault of her lips until she moaned and grabbed the front of his shirt. He deepened the touch, thrusting his tongue into her mouth, exploring greedily before pulling back.

Looking down into her face, he waited for her eyelashes to flutter open. Once they did, he was pleased to see glazed desire coursing through them. He grinned like an idiot and reluctantly pried her hands from his shirt.

"I need to get to work."

She stood there dazed, and he knew she tracked him as he walked off. He felt the heat of her stare on his ass.

Unlocking the door, he opened it and looked at her one last time.

She blinked rapidly, coming out of her trance. "Why did you do that?" She asked as she brought her fingers to her kiss-swollen lips.

"Because I wanted you to have a better memory of me." Turning, he walked through the reception area, smiled at Parvati's secretary, and whistled a tune. Boarding the elevator, he hit the floor he needed and cruised down to Jag's office.

No way could anything ruin his day now.

CHAPTER EIGHT

February 3rd – End of the work day 5pm

Colin's day was ruined. He never should have gone home the night before and let his program run. Sometime during the time he left and came back this morning, the hacker reinforced the protection on his end.

That didn't mean Colin couldn't still take the guy down, it just meant it would be longer than he expected. After that kiss this morning, he wanted to surprise Parvati and get things fixed earlier…not later.

He sighed and scrubbed his hands over his face. He didn't want to disappoint, but what the hell could he do? Pull an all-nighter and try to track the asshole down?

"You don't look too happy right now." Parvati's voice floated into the room. She didn't sound angry, only concerned.

Opening his eyes, he found her leaning against the doorframe of Jag's office. She was the best thing he'd seen since leaving her office. The cream silk sleeveless blouse showed off her toned arms. The form-fitting black skirt highlighted her slim, long legs. He could imagine them wrapped around him, her skirt pushed up around her waist; high heels still on as she rode his cock. Fuck, she was a dream to look at. She held her suit coat in her hands, and her purse was hanging by her side. She was ready to head home.

Covertly, he adjusted his growing erection, then got up from the chair he'd been sitting in for the last nine hours. He stretched and let out a tension-filled breath before heading toward her, stopping a respectable distance away. To get any closer would result in him dragging her against his body and ravishing her again. "I hate to say it, but I'm no closer to fixing this than I was when I left last night."

Her face scrunched up in displeasure, but cleared quickly. She shrugged nonchalantly, like it wasn't a big deal when he knew it was. "Do you think it will take longer to work on?"

Damn, he needed to touch her. He curled his hands into fists to keep from doing just that. "If I stay through the night, I don't think so." What the hell was he saying? He didn't want to stay overnight. At least not by himself.

"Is there anything I can do to help?"

Yes! Stay with me. "No. I'll be fine"

"Oh," she replied, disappointment lacing the single word. He was about to take it back when Jag strolled in.

"Hey, Vati, you ready to get out of here? My mom expects us in thirty." Jag went to the desk and grabbed his keys from a drawer. "You done for the night, Colin?"

"No. I'll be staying a while longer, if that's okay with you." He looked between Parvati and Jag to gauge how that would go over. He was a foreigner to the company, and he wasn't sure if they would let him hang out and work without supervision.

"That's fine," Parvati answered. "Matt can stay with you."

"Uh, actually he can't." Jag stepped up next to Colin, clutching his keys in a death grip.

Colin and Parvati both looked at him. "Why's that?" Parvati was the one to ask.

Jag's dark cheeks flushed a deep red. "I'm introducing him to Mom and Aunt Devi tonight."

Parvati practically threw herself at her cousin and screeched, making him wince. "That's fantastic!"

She squeezed Jag tightly, and Colin noticed Jag found it hard to breath. Colin peeled her arms off the poor guy, pulling her back against his side. She didn't even comment on the fact that he kept his arm across her shoulders.

"It's about time you did too. I can't believe you waited this long. You've been with him forever," she admonished.

"It's only been six months."

"Yeah, like I said, forever. You've never dated someone for that long. I knew it was serious. You two are perfect for each other. I've prayed you would find the man to compliment your soul. The Goddesses will be pleased, as well as Eros."

Colin was a bit confused at the Eros comment. The guy was a mythological Greek God. What he had to do with Jag and Matt, he didn't know. The Goddesses he understood based on Parvati and Jag's Indian culture.

"Anyway," Jag barreled on. "Maybe you should bring Colin along. You could introduce him to your mom." There was a challenge on Jag's face aimed straight at Parvati.

"No way, buddy."

A wave of disappointment unexpectedly rushed through him. He didn't know he wanted to meet her mom until the opportunity was taken away. Neither of the cousins noticed though.

"You can't use me to distract Aunt Devika. She knows you've been seeing someone for a while now. The spotlight is all yours tonight."

Jag pouted and Parvati laughed. Colin suddenly felt very lonely in the crowded room. He didn't have relationships like theirs with his cousins. He would love to be included in the warmth he felt from them. Shifting back to the desk, the cousins started bickering. He tuned it out and realized something was wrong when he lifted his head as silence descended, and he found three sets of eyes staring at him. Seemed Matt joined the party.

"What?" He asked, not sure what he'd missed.

Jag rolled his eyes and Matt poked him in the ribs. Parvati approached him, standing on the other side of the desk. "I was saying it wouldn't be a problem for you to stay here on your own. Jag and Matt trust you. I trust you."

"Great," he said, but failed to sound convincing even to his own ears.

Parvati licked her lips nervously. "And, I can come back after dinner and bring you some food. Maybe keep you company through the night."

Colin's eyes widened. He hadn't expected her offer. He couldn't have her coming back and spending the night in an uncomfortable office just so he wasn't alone. He cleared the surprise from his face and smiled. "That's okay, Parvati. It'll bore you to tears sitting up all night with me."

"You could find something else to do," Jag muttered behind his hand.

Colin shot him a glare, willing him shut up. He focused on Parvati again.

She nibbled on her lip and took a breath. "Are you sure? I don't mind. I know there is plenty of work for me to do. Besides, I don't like the thought of you toiling away here by yourself."

"That's very nice of you, but its fine. Now go. I'd say you have twenty minutes to get to that dinner."

"Oh shit," Jag grumbled. "I'll see you later, Colin. Thanks again." He shuffled Matt out the door. "Come on, Vati."

The guys left, but she didn't move. Her eyes narrowed and lips pursed. Quick as lightning, she reached across the desk, grabbed his shirt, and with more strength than he thought she had, pulled him across the desk. She planted her lips on his, kissing him soundly, and pulled back.

She smiled like a Cheshire cat and stepped backwards toward the door.

"What did you do that for?" He asked like an idiot.

She grinned. "I wanted you to have another memory of me." Spinning, she was out the door before he could process it all.

CHAPTER NINE

February 3rd – 9pm

Parvati rode the elevator up to the second floor with a smile on her face. The evening with her mother and Jag's mom had gone splendidly. Aunt Devika welcomed Matt into the family like he was her missing son. The delight in her aunt's eyes at seeing her son in love made Parvati wish she could see the same in her own mother's eyes.

Don't get her wrong. Her mom was just as thrilled for Jag as his mom, but Parvati wanted to be the one to bring her that joy. And that might explain why she was back at the office bringing Colin leftovers. God, she hoped he liked Indian food.

When Parvati started dishing up leftovers into containers and setting some of them aside, Jag gave her one of those I-know-what-you're-doing looks. The one with narrowed eyes and you're busted grin. He immediately yelled, asking his mom where the nice insulated bags were, because Parvati wanted to take food to a guy.

That drew both their moms into the kitchen. It was like

they smelled fresh meat and were animals ready to attack.

Parvati put up with the twenty questions about Colin, and kept explaining that he was working late, and she was only being nice. No one bought it. Not even her. The moms grinned at each other and began talking back and forth in Hindi. Parvati caught the words 'double wedding' and damn near fainted.

As quickly as she could extricate herself, she packed the food into a bag and beat feet out of there. Jag and Matt's laughter followed her out the door.

Now she was back at the office and nervous as hell. At least she'd had enough sense to change out of her suit at her aunt's place and get in something more comfortable. Score one for keeping a stash of clothes there. She wanted to be relaxed around the man she couldn't get out of her mind.

Taking her time walking down the hall to Jag's office, she mentally prepared for facing Colin. She discovered, quite pleasantly, thoughts of him were never far from her mind. The kiss in her office. The way he cupped her face with his big hands and slowly pulled her in with his lips. She couldn't help but respond to him.

As the doors opened and she stepped out, the silence clinging to the air settled around her. There was one distinct difference between her floor and Jag's; his had the barely audible soft rumblings of a man drifting down the hall. She followed the low cursing and settled on the doorjamb to stare at the man oblivious to her presence.

Dark eyebrows pulled together as he frowned at the screen in front of him. His lips were thinned and tugged down at the corners. He ran his hand through his wavy hair and flung himself back in his seat.

"Damn-it. Where the hell did he go?" Leaning forward again, he typed furiously on the keyboard. Shifting to his left, he concentrated on a laptop she hadn't noticed before. A few keystrokes later his eyes narrowed, then he grinned as if he'd won a toy at a carnival, turning back to Jag's computer. "Gotcha you smug bastard."

He did whatever and leaned back in the chair again. Satisfaction lit his eyes, and the curve of his mouth begged her to come kiss it.

She shifted positions and must have made a noise alerting him to her presence. His head came up and eyes zeroed in on her. Gone was the satisfied look, replaced by pure sexual hunger.

"Hey," he said getting up from his chair. He smiled at her and her tummy flipped. Damn, the man is sexy. He looked like a predator coming for its prey.

"Hey yourself," she said, holding her ground. Her voice was steadier than she thought it would be. Lust rolled through her, caressing her nerve endings, lighting them up.

When he stared at her, eyebrow lifted in question, she held out the bag for him to see. "I brought you some dinner."

His eyes widened in surprise for just a second, and she was pleased to see she could get that reaction. "You didn't have to. I told you I would be fine on my own. There was no reason for you to come back here tonight."

The comment nagged at her. Maybe he really didn't want her here.

To cover her growing unease, she shrugged and moved to the desk. Opening the bag, she focused on the contents. The thought that he was serious about her not coming back hadn't crossed her mind after the kiss in her office, or the one in Jag's right before she left. She was attracted to the man, and he seemed interested in her. She wasn't the type of woman to play coy or silly games. It was a waste of time. If they were mutually into each other, then there was no reason to beat around the bush. It wasn't her style.

"And I told you, I didn't like the idea of you being

here by yourself. Not because I don't trust you, because I do." God, could you sound any more like an idiot? "I didn't feel right having you here while Jag and I had a nice time with our family. The company is my top priority, and I need to be here for you. Um, just in case you need me to get you information or something." She paused to stop the flow of words from her mouth. She was rambling. Pulling the plate and silverware from the top of the bag, she placed it on the desk. "Plus, I was concerned about you eating. If you're anything like Jag, you'll get lost in your work and forget all about it. And I didn't to give you a code to get in, so you couldn't have gone out. Well, you could, but you wouldn't get back in. The doors automatically flip over to the security system after six."

As she rambled on, because it didn't seem like she could stop, she took out a container of Chicken Tikka Masala with rice, some Naan bread, and another container with some Papadum. She went with the most common foods they'd had that night, hoping he'd like it. She left the Gulab Jamun, golden fried Milk balls in Rose flavored syrup in and closed the bag up. Setting it off to the side, she proceeded to serve everything up. When she finished, she just stood there, unable to turn around and look at him to see the aggravation he must be feeling toward her.

Colin stepped up behind her and rested his hands on her hips. His thumbs drifted under her shirt and stroked her skin. A delighted shiver worked its way down her spine. The sparks were even more intense than the previous times he'd touched her. "I didn't mean to sound ungrateful. It was really sweet of you to think of me, and I'm glad you came back."

Like she could stop thinking about him! The barest amount of time with Colin and he invaded her brain without provocation. Trying to dive back into work this morning, all she could do was relive the cute way he stumbled and flushed with embarrassment, then proceeded to erase it from her mind with a kiss. As she sat at dinner with her family, she thought about him, here—alone. She wished he could have been there with her as her date. She wondered if he meant it when he said he was good on his own, and if he would get upset if she came back. Or if he would be pleased to see her and drop another kiss...or twenty...on her lips. Not that it mattered if he was upset. It was her place of business. She could do what she wanted.

For the love of the Goddesses, she needed her mind to stop!

*****

Colin turned Parvati around to face him. He could practically hear her mind spinning. He didn't expect her to come back, but damn was he glad she did. And not because she brought him food. He was definitely hungry, but it wouldn't be the first time he'd skipped a couple meals while working.

Her brows knit and she licked her lips. Those same soft pink lips he'd kissed earlier and was desperate to do so again. He leaned in until their lips were a breath away. "Tell me no if you don't want me to kiss you."

"I like it when you do," she said. Her voice filled with what he thought was lust. The same feeling rocketed through him.

Skimming his hands over her hips and onto her ass, he pulled her closer, fitting her pelvis against his. She was a taller woman, maybe a couple inches shorter than his six-foot frame and their bodies notched together perfectly. He had a damn good idea that she was made for him.

Physically.

Mentally.

Maybe even permanently.

Time would tell on the last part. Time he was willing to take if it was what she wanted.

He brushed his mouth over hers, waiting to feel her response. Her hands glided over his chest and around his neck. Threading her fingers in his hair at the back, she

69

put pressure on his head, nudging him closer. He got the hint. He deepened the kiss, nibbling on her lower lip. She welcomed him eagerly, tangling her tongue with his. A moan slipped free from her lips when he pulled back.

They were both breathing heavily. A dreamy expression was painted on her face. Kiss swollen lips. Mouth curved slightly at the corners. Her eyelids fluttered open and she sighed. "Why'd you stop?"

He chuckled and kissed her quickly. He needed to put some distance between them for the moment. "You were nice enough to bring me food, and I'll admit, I'm starving." He sat in his chair and pulled the plate up to him.

Inhaling deeply, the deep exotic flavors made his mouth water. Indian food wasn't something he normally went out for, but he knew this would be delicious. After the first bite, he thought about asking Parvati to marry him the second he was done eating. Amazing didn't even touch how good the food was.

He wolfed it down in a matter of minutes, along with the bread and something that looked kind of like a cracker. He didn't care what it was because, damn, it was good.

Sitting back, he patted his belly. "Best. Food. Ever."

Parvati grinned and held up the bag she brought in. "You full or do you want to try dessert? I wasn't sure what you'd like, and those were some of my favorites."

"It was great and yeah, I could eat dessert. Why don't you come over here?" He pushed back from the desk and patted his leg.

She grinned saucily before sashaying toward him. She took too long as far as he was concerned, so he grabbed her by the waist and pulled her onto his lap. A girlish giggle escaped her lips and he smiled. Contentment like he'd never felt before rolled through him. It wasn't something he was used to when it came to women. He dated but not a lot. His work took up a lot of his time and, honestly, hitting the bars and picking up random women wasn't his thing. Parvati took his mind off work, programs he tinkered with for fun, and damn near anything else that tended to swirl in the back of his mind when he was with a woman. She made him want to step away and have fun.

Once she was settled on his lap, she opened the bag and pulled out one last container. Peeling the lid off, he saw brown little donut hole looking things in a sauce. He didn't know what the hell they were, but if it was anything like the meal he'd just eaten, then he knew they would be good.

She lifted one out and held it up to his lips. Opening his mouth, he let her feed him, but before she could pull her fingers away, he closed his lips around one and sucked lightly. Cleaning all of the sugary sweet syrup away before letting her go.

As she stared at his mouth, he chewed and swallowed the sweet dessert. He smiled and plucked another one out. "My turn," he said. His voice had deepened with arousal. She parted her lips, and he placed the dessert on her tongue. Just as he'd done to her, she closed her lips on his finger and her tongue swirled around the digit. She gripped his wrist and pulled him from her mouth. Quickly chewing, she swallowed down the little donut then sucked his finger back in to the second knuckle. With a firm lock on his wrist, she mimicked what it would be like fucking her lush mouth. In and out, one by one she sucked him. He could only imagine what the action would feel like on his dick.

She turned on his lap to straddle him, and he was grateful Jag's chair didn't have arms. He'd wondered about it when he was working the day before. It was odd, but he could see the charm of the armless seat now.

Grinding against Colin, Parvati continued to devour him finger by finger. Her eyes glazed and lids partially closed. She was enjoying their foreplay as much as he was. The pulse in her neck picked up the more she moved her body over his. The heat of her core branded him through the barrier of their clothes. His cock pushed against the zipper of his jeans with each hitch of her hips. Desperate to get closer to her.

He slipped his free hand under her shirt, skimming over her velvety dark skin. He didn't stop until he cupped a breast. Rubbing his thumb across her nipple, it hardened and she moaned. He pinched and she bucked. Every action was rewarded with a sensual reaction.

Fuck, he needed inside her. He popped his finger free from her mouth and grabbed her by the hips. Forcing her to stand, he quickly unbuttoned her jeans. She moved back as he pulled them off with her help, dragging her panties with them.

Before he fucked her, he wanted to hear her scream out his name. Tugging her forward, he had her straddle his thighs again. Spreading his legs, he had her sit closer to his knees, leaving space for him to play. When he got her how he wanted, he pulled her top off and unhooked her bra. Where the clothes landed he didn't have a clue. He was lost in the vision before him. Creamy, caramel skin. Full, pert breasts tipped with brown beaded nipples. Her dark hair flowed over her shoulder and she brushed it aside.

"Damn you're beautiful," he whispered in awe.

"Thanks, now I want to see you." She reached for the button on his jeans, and he batted her hands away.

"Not yet. I'll lose it if you touch me."

She pouted, sticking out her lower lip. Lunging for it, he sucked it into his mouth. Her hands trailed over his shoulders and gripped the back of his shirt. She pulled and he sat back, allowing her to take it off.

Her hungry gaze ate him up. "Damn you're hot! I love the way your shirts cling to your chest but this…holy hell." She wiggled her eyebrows and he chuckled.

Running his hands up her legs, he aimed straight for her neatly trimmed pussy. He ran a hand through the curls

72

and over her sensitive lips. She shuddered and arched, thrusting her breasts out, practically begging him to suckle them. Leaning forward, he captured a nipple with his mouth while he teased her with his hand. He alternated between dipping inside and swirling with his fingers around her clit. She started bouncing on his hand, his palm pressed to her clit, his fingers thrusting in and out of her tight core. Her moans grew louder, nails dug into his back. He could feel how close she was, the slight rippling of her inner muscles. It didn't take much longer before she came apart, screaming his name.

He reached for the zipper on his pants to free himself when he stopped. He didn't have a condom. He hadn't planned on fucking her, or anyone for that matter, so he didn't carry any with him.

He groaned and his head fell back.

"What?"

"No condom," he said, refusing to look at her satiated face. If he did, he might beg for relief.

He felt her moving on his lap. A drawer opened then closed. He peeked at what she was doing. A cocky little grin kicked up one side of her mouth, and she waved a small square package at him. "No problem."

"Do I even want to know why there are condoms in the drawer, and how you know about them?"

She shrugged and unbuttoned his jeans, then gingerly pulled the zipper down. Reaching inside his pants, she gripped his shaft and a delighted little 'oh' burst from her mouth. Masculine pride had him sitting up straight.

"My what big," she paused as he helped push his jeans out of the way and she pulled his cock out. "Hands you have." Ripping open the package, she rolled it on him. Scooting up his body, with the aid of his hands on her ass, she slid along his erection. The hard, heavy width stroking over her wet pussy lips. They both groaned, and he was dying for her to plunge down on him.

She wiggled, gripped his shaft and without ceremony, dropped down on his throbbing member. Colin's head hit the back of the chair as sheer bliss exploded within him. The tight walls of her pussy clung. Flexing around his shaft. He was in absolute heaven.

They had gone from him being an utter ass to her riding him slowly, nails digging into his shoulders in the span of a day. It was amazing.

There was a connection between them, something telling him he needed more of her and not just skin-to-skin contact. But hell, this was fucking good too. Nimble, delicate fingers dug into his shoulders as she picked up her rhythm.

He took one her of nipples into his mouth and sucked on it hard. She bucked and moaned. Her pussy rippled, so he did it again. Switching from one breast to the other, her breathy moans increased. She moaned his name and he prayed she was close. He refused to come until she had again.

"That's it, Vati. Come all over my dick. Pull me under with you."

He helped her out with his hands on her ass. Lifting her and letting her drop back down with force. It felt too fucking good, and he wouldn't last much longer. Thankfully, Parvati came, screaming him name. He picked her up and let her fall back on his dick a couple more times before he followed her into bliss. He shouted her name and collapsed back in the chair. Parvati plastered to his front.

Minutes passed by and the only sounds in the room were their breathing and the hum of the computers. Eventually, Parvati pushed up off his chest to lean back. A contented smile stretched her beautiful face.

"Now, that's a dessert," she hummed.

Colin couldn't help but chuckle. "I'm going to have to have another taste." Leaning forward he captured her lips again in another sensual assault. He could really get used to doing this.

CHAPTER TEN

February 4th – 8am

Jag pulled into the office garage and was surprised to see Parvati's car parked in her usual spot. Pulling up in the space next to it, he shut the engine off and looked over at Matt. "She couldn't have stayed all night, could she?"

"Your guess is as good as mine. We never heard from Colin or your sister after dinner. Maybe she got caught up in work and decided to sleep in her office."

Jag didn't believe that. Not his cousin. She always made it a point to go home and get cleaned up for the next day. She insisted on presenting the most professional look as possible. Long nights were no excuse for being in the same outfit looking ragged. "No. She probably came in early to get some work done. You know how much she's been stressed over the hacker." Feeling better about that theory, he got out of his car and touched the hood of hers. His brows furrowed. "It's cold."

Matt laughed and grabbed him by the arm. "Let's go find out what she's been up to then. I bet its something good."

Stepping into the elevator, he didn't know which floor to press. Did he go to his office to see if Colin was still there or if he'd left a note? Or did he head one more floor up and see if his cousin was in her office frantically working.

Matt made the decision for him. Pressing the button for their floor, he leaned back against the wall. "Might as well check your office first. That way, if she's in hers, you'll have something to take to her when you barge in. That is, I'm assuming Colin would have left you a note or something about the fix."

"Yeah," Jag mumbled, a thread of concern bleeding through. His cousin never stayed overnight at work. She would go home no matter how late she worked. One or two times, when the company first started, he would leave for the night and come back in the morning to see her right where he left her. She would freak out, telling him to cover for her so she could pop home for a quick shower and change of clothes. It never took her longer than an hour to do it all.

The elevator pinged and they stepped out. Jag stood still for a second, listening for any noise. He didn't hear anything. Nothing was out of the ordinary as they stood in the hall.

Matt rolled his eyes and grabbed his hand. They walked to his office together and when they stepped into it, Jag was ever so grateful Matt held his hand tightly. Otherwise, the shock of what he'd seen would have brought him to his knees.

Parvati and Colin were huddled together, Parvati sitting on Colin's lap, her lips pressed to his ear. Jag blinked a couple of times — he stood corrected. It was a partially naked Colin his cousin was sitting on. Jag didn't know about the bottom half, but he hoped like hell the man was wearing pants while sitting in his chair.

Matt cleared his throat, bringing both their heads up.

Parvati, the cheeky woman, grinned and finger waved.

Colin turned beet red. His fair complexion easily showing his embarrassment.

As Matt and Jag made their way further into the room, Jag was yet again caught off guard by a stack of wrappers sitting on his desk. Gold, metallic squares, which could be only one thing.

"You had sex in my office?" he blurted out.

Parvati and Matt had the nerve to laugh. Jag looked between the two, but it was Parvati who spoke.

"It isn't the first time it's happened in this room."

"Oh my god, you've had sex in my office before." Jag's voice rose to near hysteria. Panic at knowing way too much about her rose in his throat, threatening to cut off his air supply.

Parvati rolled her eyes at him and stood up. She picked up Colin's shirt from somewhere on the floor and handed it to him. "Don't be such a drama queen, Jagjit. You have sex in here with Matt all of the time."

"That doesn't mean you get to!"

Parvati turned on him, shooting an imperious look his way. Her back stiffened, left eyebrow rose, and her lips thinned. "Actually, since this is my building and company, I can do whatever the hell I please. If that means I want to fuck Colin in every room of this place, then I will."

Something happened then that had never happened before, and Jag could only chalk it up to his cousin being a true descendant of the Goddess Parvati and all of her incarnations. A thread of energy pulsed from her and spread over Jag. He stepped back once before wobbly dropping to his knees.

As Jag struggled to keep his head up, he noticed Colin run a hand down her back. He leaned over and whispered something in her ear that made her smile. The energy pulse stopped, and Jag finally felt he could stand up.

Matt looked down at him confused, and reached out a hand to help him up. Jag took it like a man about to drown.

He shook off the intense feeling that settled over him and let out a deep breath. "I forget sometimes the power you have. I'm sorry to have offended you, Parvati. It won't happen again."

Parvati smirked and brushed the foil packets into the trash. "Don't forget it again," she quipped.

At that point, she forgave all. Normally, she would have gone off in a rage, but she didn't appear angry.

"Forget what?" Matt asked, clearly not catching on to what had happened.

Jag looked at his boyfriend and then at Colin. They were pure human. Not a bit of Mystic in either of them. He'd have to explain it later, since he didn't know how much Colin knew of the others roaming the planet. "I'll tell ya later, babe," he said before kissing Matt on the cheek.

Parvati threaded her fingers with Colin's. As they walked by, trashcan in tow, she kissed Jag on the cheek. "We'll talk later."

He looked down at the trashcan she was holding, then back at her smiling face.

"I'm not sure I want to know," he chuckled. Seeing her happy had his heart singing.

"You don't, but I do need to replace your stash." Laughing, she left the room, Colin right behind her, laptop tucked against his side. It looked like his cousin had finally found the one. He only hoped it would last.

CHAPTER ELEVEN

February 6th – 8am

Parvati rolled to a stop in her parking space at work with a smile permanently etched on her face. For the past few nights, she had been staying late with Colin as he worked out the hacker problem. They didn't get into the details of what happened, but he'd told her that today would be the day they brought the main site back up, and new security measures would be put in place as well.

He still had work to do in the office, and that was what had her grinning like a fool. She would get to spend more time with him before they were forced to figure out what came next. She knew what she wanted—more time with him that didn't involve work. She was falling in love with him, and she wondered if he felt the same. It didn't matter to her that she had known him for only a couple of days. She was a freaking Goddess of love and devotion. If she didn't know what it felt like to fall in love, then she needed a new title.

After the night she brought him dinner, they decided on a similar arrangement. She would leave work, do whatever she had scheduled with her family, then she would bring him leftovers and they would spend time together. And not just having sex. Though that did happen quite a few more times and, no, not in Jag's office. The drama queen was still throwing a fit over that, and even ordered a new office chair. Good thing she brought his old one to her own office.

Parvati moved Colin from where he'd been, to hers. There was more room, and it was easy enough to set up another terminal for him to use. They enjoyed good conversation or sitting in silence. He understood she needed to work, and she knew he needed to do the same. They worked well side by side. Plus, she had that wonderful couch waiting to be used. A couple of mid-afternoon breaks helped them both re-center and recharge.

A light tap on her window pulled her from her musings. The object of her affection stood next to her car. The corners of his mouth pulled up into a devastating grin and she sighed. A lock of hair drifted onto his forehead, and she had the urge to brush it aside.

Turning the engine off, she climbed out of her car, tea in hand and purse over her shoulder. Colin leaned in close as she shut the door, edging her backwards. Grabbing the cup from her hand, he placed it on the roof, cupped her face with his big hands and brushed his mouth against hers. Light and leisurely, the soft kisses made her heart beat out of control. The man seduced her with a mere touch of his lips.

Too soon the kissing ended. Her eyes fluttered open to see him standing there with banked heat in his eyes. "I missed you this morning. You should have come home with me last night."

Parvati flushed. They may have shared a lot of intimacies in her office, but being in his home would be entirely different. She wanted to go, but not until the site was back up and he wasn't technically working for her. There was this need for him to want her there because he wanted it, not because he spent the entire day with her and

81

didn't know how to not invite her. She wanted him to pick her and not out of convenience. "You know I couldn't."

"No, I only know that you said you couldn't and didn't tell me why. Do you have some strange nightly ritual I don't know about? Do you rub goop all over you face, put cucumbers on your eyes, and stay in one position the entire night when you sleep?" He plucked her drink up off the roof and handed it to her. Threading their fingers together, he tugged to get them walking.

She chuckled lightly. "No. Nothing strange." Her nose scrunched up thinking about it. "Who does that still? I thought the whole night cream and cucumbers thing went out of nightly fashion years ago."

Colin shrugged. "Not night cream. I think it has cucumbers and oatmeal in it now. I'd have to ask my mom."

"Your mom?" It was the first time he'd mentioned his mother. So far the bulk of their conversations revolved around them, not the people who raised them.

"She still does it. She and her best friend try out all sorts of age-defying concoctions. The cinnamon mask didn't go over very well. She said there was a burning sensation that was pretty uncomfortable."

"Oh dear. That doesn't sound good." They stepped into the elevator and he hit the button for their floor. Once he did, he turned around and crowded her against the back wall. Resting his hands on either side of her face, he leaned in close and kissed her. It wasn't like before. It wasn't soft and teasing. No, it was soul-searing and breath-stealing. He licked the seam of her lips, and she let him in. Tongues tangled, teeth clashed. He nipped her bottom lip before sucking it into his mouth.

She moaned and reached for him with her free hand. She wanted to feel his body pressed tight to hers. Feel the heat of his skin, the beat of his heart. But he stepped back, a dopey lopsided grin on his face. There was a ping and the door slid open. One of her employees stepped in, looked at the both of them and stepped back out. His muttered 'sorry' was cut off by the door closing.

"That was awkward."

"Maybe for him. Not for me." He licked his lips. "I want to ask you something."

Her heart sped up and breath stopped up in her lungs. He sounded so serious and, in turn, it made her nervous. "Okay," she squeaked out.

"Would you be my date for a Valentine's party?"

Parvati blinked a couple of times. That wasn't what she expected him to ask. She blew out a breath. "A Valentine's party? Whose?"

This time Colin blushed. "My mom's. It's the annual Patterson Paramour Party. She's invited every single woman she knows — and a few men. I thought I could cut off her matchmaking if I brought a date."

Her heart sunk. "Oh," she said numbly. "When is it?"

"Saturday the 14th."

"On Valentine's Day, of course."

"She's really excited about it, and I don't want to disappoint her by not going. I sure as hell don't want to be the prized bull being sold at auction though."

She frowned when she didn't follow his line of thought.

"I don't need to be paraded around to all the single ladies."

"So you're looking for a single guy?"

"Not funny. I don't swing that way. I thought you would know that by now." He wiggled his eyebrows and she couldn't help but roll her eyes. He dipped his head to kiss her again, but she turned her head away at the last second.

"So, that's it? You need a date for a party so you don't have to spend the entire time getting hit on? You could have just asked. There was no need to try and seduce me into going. I would have been happy to help out."

Colin's expression turned to confusion. The elevator pinged, door slid open, and she ducked under his arm and walked out.

Anger at being played a fool fueled her as she went down the hall. People in her path stepped aside without a word. Even Stacy, who was magically at her desk already, didn't bother to stop her.

*****

The door to elevator slid closed, snapping him from the dazed state he was in. What the hell just happened? He smashed the button to open the door back up, but it was too late. The elevator descended and he was stuck riding it back down to the garage. He should have taken the stairs but that would have wasted even more time trying to find the damn things. Heading back to Parvati's floor, he tried to figure out what went wrong.

He'd greeted her at her car because he'd missed her like crazy. Just like he told her.

He'd kissed her, just like he wished he could have when he woke up that morning alone in his bed.

He'd gotten her into the elevator and kissed her again because he craved another taste of her.

He'd invited her to his mother's party because he wanted her there…wait, that wasn't how it came out though was it?

Replaying the words over in his head, he finally figured it out. She must have thought he only wanted her there to deflect his mom, when that was the farthest thing from his mind. He needed to remedy this and quick.

Parvati was not the kind of woman to let it go. Once you made it on her shit list, it took an act of divine intervention to get off of it. He'd gotten lucky the first time around. He didn't think he'd fair that well a second time. Just look at that poor sap that hacked her company. He would be paying heavily for what he did…and soon. Colin had heard her talking to the investigator and her lawyer about it all.

As soon as the elevator door opened, he was out like the hounds of hell were on his heels. He breezed through the call center, passed the glass offices and break room, and didn't bother stopping for Stacy. He reached for the knob of Parvati's door when Stacy's words stopped him.

"I wouldn't do that if I were you. She's pissed and liable to rip a couple limbs or one in particular, off." She looked down at his crotch and smirked.

"We had a misunderstanding."

Stacy let loose an unladylike snort. "Yeah, I doubt that. Vati doesn't get meanings crossed. She's pretty good at sorting through the bullshit."

"I hate to break it to you little dragon, but she didn't understand what I was saying. I'm going to straighten her out."

"I could shoot your ass with a fireball if you try to go in there."

He turned and pinned her with a glare. "Do it and see what happens."

They scowled at each other for only a couple seconds when Stacy broke eye contact. "How did you know what I was? Why is it you make me nervous?"

Colin shrugged. He didn't know how he knew. He just did. That little incident in Jag's office when Jag dropped to his knees in front of Parvati; Colin felt something whip through the air. He instinctively knew he needed to soothe her, to calm her down.

Since Colin and Parvati shared their first touch, he'd become more aware of things that shouldn't be. Things that he thought didn't exist, existed. It didn't freak him out either. He went with the flow of it all and accepted what could be, and actually was.

Stacy tilted her head to the side and studied him in open frankness. "It's because of Parvati, isn't it? You're her destined love; therefore, you get the gift of understanding. You can now see what the mere human cannot."

"Yes," he said with confidence.

"Well, you better fix this misunderstanding then. She's deserves happiness and to be loved for everything she is."

Colin nodded. "Cancel all of her morning appointments then." He faced the door again, took a deep breath and opened the door.

Parvati, who sat at her desk, stiffened. "Go away, Mr. Patterson."

"No."

"I can make you leave." Her eyes narrowed angrily.

He snorted. He may be a geek, but he wasn't a pushover. "Come over here and try it." He crossed his arms over his chest and waited.

"Ugh," she grunted out. "I don't know why I bother with you men. Always a disappointment."

"That's not what you said last night when I fucked you on the desk. Or when you rode me hard until you collapsed, barely able to keep your eyes open from sheer bliss. You also didn't sound disappointed when I spread you out like a feast, and kissed and licked every inch of your delicious skin. You screamed my name as you came on my tongue and fingers."

"So crude, Mr. Patterson. Apparently, it was something to pass the time, nothing more."

"You know it's more than that. Every minute I'm with you, I pray for more. Every second I'm away; I'm dying inside, aching to be with you. Jesus woman, I've known you all of four days, and already I can't imagine my life without you."

He strode across the room to a very stunned Parvati. Her mouth opened and closed like a fish trying to breath. Her face had gone pale. Plucking her up from her chair, he carried her to the couch, sitting down with her on his lap. Snaking an arm around her waist, he anchored her to him. There was no way she was leaving or moving away from him unless he wanted her to.

"You heard me wrong in the elevator."

She opened her mouth to protest, he was sure, so he drove on.

"No, I misspoke in the elevator. I asked you to the party because I want you there. I asked you to be my date because I can't imagine finding or going with anyone else. I cherish being with you. Talking to you. Laughing with you. Sitting in complete silence with you. I fucking adore you. There is no one else I would rather be with."

Her pink lips wobbled, and a sheen of tears reflected in her dark eyes. He kissed her gently, and then rested his forehead against hers. Touching her calmed him down. Soothed the ragged edges of his nerves. The instant flare of panic he felt when she fled receded as she melted into him.

"I want to introduce you to my mom and tell her to stop matchmaking. I've found my One. I don't care how long we've known each other because I'm falling in love with you. Your strength. Your commitment to this company and your family. Your beautiful spirit that believes everyone deserves to find that special someone. You're that person for me. My special someone who sings to my soul and soothes me just by being there. You're my perfect match."

"Oh, Colin," she sighed, the warmth of her breath ghosting over his lips. The puff of air sent a shiver down his frame. His dick twitched, and he willed it to not fill, not that it was doing any good. This was a serious conversation. There would be plenty of time for convincing her how much he adored her later.

She put her hands on the sides of his face and leaned back to look him in the eyes. Radiant warmth glittered in their depths. "You're my special someone too."

CHAPTER TWELVE

February 14th – 5pm

Parvati fidgeted in the passenger seat of Colin's car, as he walked around the front of it. Nervous excitement swept through her blood. After the night was over, they planned on heading back to his house. Her overnight bag was stashed in the trunk; and any time she looked at him, a giddy little giggle tried to escape. It felt like prom night all over again. A stolen night away, but this time with the man she loved. It would be her first time staying at his place. A first time either of them had spent the entire night cuddled up in each other's arms.

After that ridiculous misunderstanding on her part, and his failure to tell her exactly what he meant, they eased back from their intense draw. They had only known each other a couples days, and as much as she wanted to dive in head first, they both decided they needed to spend time together outside of work. They needed to give the relationship some breathing room.

Tonight would be their first outing as a couple. His parents would finally see them together and all of those single women—and handful of men—would have their hearts broken.

Damn, she hoped it went like she imagined.

Colin opened her door and held out a hand. She took it and allowed him to pull her to her feet. Wrapping an arm around her waist, he kissed her quickly on the lips. "It's going to be great."

Those ice-blue eyes of his stared down adoringly into her face. The corners of his mouth curved up, and she couldn't resist kissing him again. Contact with his lips made her brain melt and her legs turn to jelly. His firm mouth worked across her soft ones. His tongue came out to swipe across and she opened automatically. The sound of a door opening and raucous laughter had them breaking apart.

"Later," he rumbled. "You and me in my big ass bed for as long as I want. I'm going to love every inch of your body until you scream the bloody house down."

A shiver worked down her spine at his words. Her nipples beaded and pussy throbbed. Surprisingly enough, she no longer felt nervous about meeting his mom and dad. He would be meeting her family the next day at brunch. That's how serious they were about each other—after almost two weeks.

"Let's get this party started so I can get you home and have my way with you."

Home. She liked the sound of that. Linking their hands together, they walked slowly to the community center.

Lights shone from every window. Little hearts decorated each one. Music pulsed from one end of the L-shaped building, and she could see people milling about.

"Your mom really goes all out for this, doesn't she? What's she going to do when she finds out you're already taken?"

A wolfish grin lit his face. "So, you're staking a claim on me tonight?"

"You know it. I don't play around, Colin. I know when its right. It's what I do for a living."

He stopped them before they reached the door. He turned her as he faced her. His blue eyes searched her face. "And is it? Are you sure?"

"What I feel for you?"

He nodded.

"Definitely. I'm in love with you. I probably have been from the start...when you said I was a tyrant."

"I told you I was sorry about that."

She got up on tiptoes and kissed his nose. "I know. It amazed me that I wasn't calling for your head on a platter."

Colin wrapped his arms around her and pulled her close. His body pressed to her, she felt his heavy erection pressed against her belly. A responding throb of need had her squeezing her thighs together. Dipping his head he kissed her, thrusting his tongue into her mouth. Gone was his usual sensual slide into decadence.

She looped her arms around his neck, weaving her hands into his hair. She sucked his tongue and he groaned, the sound vibrating against her hardening nipples.

Vaguely she heard a door open and loud laughter.

A woman gasped. "Colin Thomas Patterson, what are you doing to that woman?"

A deep male voice chuckled. "It looks like he's kissing her, Meggie. Want me to remind you what that feels like?"

Colin ended the kiss and stepped back. Shock and disgust written all over his face. "Dad!"

From what Parvati could make out, Colin's mom blushed as his dad laughed boisterously. She couldn't help but join in.

Shaking his head, Colin slung his arm over her shoulders and pulled her next to him. "Mom. Dad. This is Parvati. You're future daughter-in-law."

Colin's mom rushed forward and enveloped Colin in a hug. His dad followed behind, a grin plastered on his face. "Welcome to the family," he said as he folded her into his arms.

"I haven't been asked yet," she mumbled into the older man's chest.

"Eh, that's a little thing," he said, a wry smile on his face. "My boy won't take long getting you to commit. Once he sets his mind on something, he generally gets what he wants."

When they both stepped back, Colin's mom switched places with his dad and hugged her tight. As the older woman stepped back, she held onto Parvati's arms and looked at Colin while smiling serenely. "I knew you needed the right incentive." She looked back at Parvati, and she could see tears gathering in the other woman's eyes. "She's stunning. I can't wait for you two to give me grandbabies."

Parvati's eyes rounded, and his dad knew to pull the woman away.

Colin wrapped his other arm around her and dropped a kiss on her head. "Don't worry, you'll get used to them," he whispered.

She laughed and they all looked at her quizzically. "Wait until you meet my family."

Colin's eyes rounded and she laughed. "Don't worry," she repeated his words. "You'll get used to them."

Colin's mom and dad, Thom as she later learned he

liked to be called, swept them inside and proceeded to show off the newly minted couple.

EPILOGUE

February 15th – 10am

Chloe stood in front of her scrying bowl, window open with a light breeze blowing the skirt of her chiton around her legs. The soft scent of freesia floated on the late morning air. She dipped an obsidian stone into the dark glass bowl filled with rainwater. The water rippled gently as she removed it and a drip fell from the tip, just as she'd intended. Taking in a deep breath then letting it out, she focused her thoughts on the couple she was pulling together in the latest challenge. With gentle strokes, she ran the obsidian around the edge of the bowl over and over again, waiting for it to resonate and large circular ripples to form, moving from the outer rim to the middle.

Her sisters thought she'd lost her mind for water scrying. Saying it was an old and ridiculous art. That the viewer saw only what they wanted and nothing about it was real. Chloe shook her head at them and secretly smiled whenever they got on her case.

Over the centuries of her life she perfected the art. Learned to look into the past, present and future. She even took the time to look at the lives of her sisters. Saw the paths they were on with those currently in their lives. She never told them what she saw. It was information she kept to herself, using it when they became too full of themselves. Enjoying the glimmer of surprise when things worked out exactly as she predicted.

The only person scrying didn't work on was the person wielding the power. She had no idea if Eros was to be hers. If all of the trouble and heartache she was currently going through would pay off in the end, or if she was wasting her time. At one point, she thought to trick the All Seeing Eye and look at Eros, but it too proved futile. He was shown in the three states of being, but all aspects she was involved in were missing. The meetings they'd already had. The meetings they'd arranged in the future. All of the run-ins over the years, she was nowhere to be seen in the visions.

The water's fast rippling surface brought to life Parvati and Colin in Parvati's family home. Her family, to include the newest boyfriend Matt, surrounded them talking…laughing…enjoying life. Leaning back against her chaise, Chloe tuned into the scene like it was her favorite show on television. She may be ancient but that didn't mean she wasn't up on the times. She stayed abreast of the mortal realm and the advances they made. It was humorous to her, much like what was happening in the depths of the bowl.

*****

On the mortal realm…

Parvati pulled Colin into the kitchen under the ruse of having him help her bring out food to the table. Already, thirty minutes after arriving at her family home, her mother monopolized Colin, peppering him with questions about their engagement (they weren't) and their wedding (not even close to being a thought). Parvati hadn't gotten a word in edgewise and had even been shooed off by her mother. To say the woman was happy about the development in Parvati's life would be an understatement.

Reclining against the counter, she pulled Colin in close; sliding her hands up his well-defined chest. A smile lit his face as he caged her in, placing his hands on the counter on either side of her. "I don't know why you thought to warn me about your family. There's nothing wrong with them. They haven't done anything my parents haven't already said or plotted."

"Says the man I haven't been able to get near for the last half hour."

"Jealous already? I can see where you'd feel threatened. Your mom is hot just like you but in an older more mature way. And she cooks like a dream. I could live happily on those little donut balls." He chuckled and kissed her on the forehead.

"Gulab Jamun." She sighed and looped her arms around his waist, pulling his body flush with hers. "At least get the name right," she said and rested her head on his chest. His arms came around her, tucking her closer to his body.

She sighed again, this time with contentment. Everything about Colin eased her yearning for someone to call her own. He soothed her restless soul and gave her a sense of peace she didn't think she would ever find.

The night before, after the party with his parents, they went back to his place, snuggled on the couch and talked about the evening. Laughing at the disappointment of the men who came hoping to hook up with him, and seeing their abject horror when the twins from Colin's childhood decided to pursue them.

They spent the midnight hours making love, sleeping in each other's arms, then waking up to do it all over again. In the morning, she woke up to find her overnight bag completely empty and her toiletries placed neatly next to his in the bathroom; like they had always been there. Her clothes had been put away in a newly emptied drawer. They had yet to talk about it; but, based on what she discovered that morning, Colin wanted her to move in with him. She didn't have any objections to it, but she did want to be asked.

With an ease she had never expected to experience, they slipped into their relationship like they had always been together.

"Colin, Parvati," her mother's dulcet voice called out. The light patter of her feet on the tile flooring proceeded her entering the kitchen.

Colin stepped back, putting unwanted distance between them. Parvati wanted his arms to always be around her. He turned a mega-watt grin onto her mother. "Mrs. Amata, what can I help you with?"

Parvati's mom blushed and waved her hand in the air. "You will call me Devi for now. Once you marry my daughter, you will call me sasa. It means mother-in-law. Now come with me. Since you and my daughter have not brought the food out, we will look at baby pictures." She wrapped her arm around his and started taking him from the room. "You and my daughter will make lots of beautiful grandchildren for me. Beautiful, dark haired babies, with your mesmerizing blue eyes. I'd like that. They will be brilliant and unique like you both. The best of your brains and her beauty. All of my friends will be jealous."

Colin glanced back at her with a look of panic in his eyes. Parvati raised an eyebrow and smirked. "You wanted her."

"Uhh…." Colin's words, if he was even going to find them, were cut off by her mother.

"You will give me twins. The Goddess Parvati will grant that wish." Her mother looked over her shoulder at Parvati. "You will call to her, yes?"

The smile that ghosted her lips at Colin's wide-eyed panic, dropped. Her pulse picked up, heart beating rapidly in her chest. Oh goddess! She wanted children, but from the sound of it, her mother wanted many. "Umm…I don't know if she honors those requests."

"Posh! She will for you. For her namesake. The Goddess of love and devotion should have twins. After them, there will be more grandchildren for me. Your family will like that, won't they, Colin?"

Colin and Parvati exchanged looks. Equally panicked. Equally surprised at the direction of the visit. Moments passed between them before Colin grinned. "They would and I'm sure Vati and I will give it our best shot."

Her mother giggled like a schoolgirl, then let go of Colin's arm, leaving the kitchen. He turned around and lifted Parvati off the floor. "We'll have a damn good time trying," he said before crushing his lips against hers in a heated kiss.

"Yeah, we will," she agreed, threading her fingers through his hair, she kissed him again.

*****

Chloe dipped her finger in the scrying bowl, disturbing the image of Parvati and Colin making out in her mother's kitchen. They would have a good life together. She could feel it in her bones.

A slow grin curled up her lips, as a sense of satisfaction threaded through her.

She'd beaten Eros again, matching up his precious minion and her human. He didn't need to know she'd brought down one of his pet projects to get it done either. It had been the most logical thing to do in order to bring Parvati and Colin together.

She now had a full two weeks to hold over his head. Two weeks to give her leverage for the next month's couple. Hopefully, it would be a challenge. Something she could get more involved with. She couldn't wait until they met up again.

THE END

Thane: January
Mystic Zodiac, Book 1

Fallen Angel Thane has been exiled to the realm of humans and Mystics for almost fifty years after what he considers a slight *misunderstanding*, too bad Zeus didn't agree. After the blush of exile wears off, Thane dedicates his new life to helping those in need, all in the hope of impressing the imposing God.

A visit from his Watcher with one more task sets Thane up to finally get what he's dreamed about for decades… his rightful place back on Olympus with his brothers. All he needs to do is keep one woman from "doing something stupid." He determined to ignore his body responding for the first time in almost fifty years in order to go home.

Amara Hope is desperate to bring her brother home, traveling into the heart of Viral City day after day putting her life at risk. As her last living relative, he's all she has left. When a hunky Good Samaritan grudgingly offers help, she's all too willing to accept. Once they get her brother home and begin spending more time together, the more Amara knows he's the one for her.

What the two don't know is that the Gods are playing games with their lives, and they're on a collision course with love.

Word Count: 32,299

Parvati: February
Mystic Zodiac, Book 2

Parvati Shiva, a true descendent of the Goddess of love and devotion, is fed up. She runs a successful dating site, connecting Mystics and humans all over the world with their one true love. The only she hasn't been able to find love for is...her.

When a hacker gets into her network and website, shutting down her site in the height of the busy season, she calls on her cousin Jag for help, who in turn reaches out to an old friend.

Colin Patterson, IT guru and confirmed bachelor, quickly agrees to help his friend's sister out with her computer problem, hoping it will be a long drawn out process. He's eager to escape his mother's matchmaking Valentine's Day party. She's invited all of the single women — and a few men — to jump-start his dating life, something he has no interest in at all.

One mistaken identity later, Colin ruins his chance with the beautiful Indian woman he's instantly attracted to. Will he be able to prove he isn't a boss bashing idiot, save Parvati's company, and win her affections before he doesn't have a reason to stick around?

Warning: This book contains a geeky hero who can't keep his mouth shut, a strong willed businesswoman dealing in love, and an attraction that neither can deny.

Please note: **This book has a hot M/M scene.**

Word Count: 26,817

Currently available in ebook only

Shifted Plans
Shifter U, Book 1

Decadent Publishing

Avery Hillman has one year of college left. Once it's over she has plans, BIG plans. A job managing her family's medical practice, an apartment of her own, and a new life where she's the one in charge. No hovering family, no annoying siblings, and no mate to have to divide her time to be with.

Declan Weller has one more class to finish. One more thing he can cross off his ten-year plan. Once that is done, he can transfer to the new job waiting for him and his new life. He isn't looking for his mate and as far as he's concerned, finding her can wait another two years.

The Fates have a plan of their own. One that includes throwing Avery and Declan in each other's path. It's high time those two found each other and learn the most important thing of all…sometimes plans need to shift.

~~~~~

Genre: Paranormal Romance, New Adult, Shifters
Featuring Lion Shifters

Word Count: 27,796

Available in ebook and print

Craving More
Tiger Nip, Book 1

TEZ Publishing

Corrine Hart is ready for few days off for rest and relaxation. At the top of her to-do list is spending as much time as possible in tiger form and doing her best to banish all thoughts of the mysterious Hunky Cupcake Guy who spent the last two weeks driving her libido insane.

Jett Montgomery-Murphy just wants to know if the tasty treats that keep showing up at work are the same ones his best friend used to get while they were in college. A trip out to Sweet Confections confirms what he thought and brings him in close contact with the one woman he's secretly lusted after for years, his best friend's sister Corrine.

A late night tryst leads to two tigers finding their mates and two humans unsure what to do next. Add in an overbearing brother, a best friend with her own drama, and a crazy ex-girlfriend that has a checkered past and you have a recipe for disaster.

Will Corrine and Jett be able to overcome the unexpected obstacles on their way to falling in love? Or will they throw in the towel before the relationship even gets off the ground?

~~~~~
Genre: Paranoraml Romance, Shifters
Featuring Tiger Shifter

*Word Count: 47,309*

Available in ebook and print

## Claiming More
Tiger Nip, Book 2

TEZ Publishing

Sampson Hart has known Mary Jane Poppy for ten years. She's his sister's best friend, business partner, and has had a crush on Sam for years. When the mating pull hits him, he's ready to claim her as his own. Given their history, it should be simple. Right?

MJ has loved Sam since she was fifteen. But being a hybrid, she's been told all her life she won't have a mate. When Sam proclaims she belongs to him, she doesn't believe it; the mating pull isn't there, and Sam isn't meant to be hers.

Running back home to escape the love she feels for Sam, MJ agrees to become the companion of a man who lost his mate and has three young children to raise. It is the only way to set Sam free to find the one he is truly meant to be with.

Will Sam be Claiming More or will the one he desires the most find comfort in the arms of another?

~~~~~
Genre: Paranoraml Romance, Shifters
Featuring Tiger Shifter

Word Count: 58,101

Available in ebook and print

Dallas & Kacie: Tiger Bite
Tiger Nip, Book 2.5

TEZ Publishing

It's the holiday season and Kacie Cook is counting down the hours until its time to close up Sweet Confections. Not that she has any great plans for the week the bakery is closed. She won't be seeing her family — yet again, and all of her friends are too busy. All she has planned is a little rest and relaxation. That is until the last customer of the night walks in. Could he be the one to bring some holiday cheer and possibly change her life forever?

~~~~~

Genre: Paranoraml Romance, Shifters
Featuring Tiger Shifter

Word Count: 15,773

ABOUT THE AUTHOR

 Brandy is a paranormal romance author who, on occasion, likes to dabble with contemporary. She's addicted to MDK shows and who-done-its. You'll almost never see her without some type of skull paraphernalia on and is always dreaming of more tattoos.

Brandy is a Navy brat, prior enlisted Army, current Army wife, and mom. She lives in Virginia with her husband of almost 20 years, their three kids and one dog.

Brandy is all over the web. Pick one or all to keep up with her.

Don't forget to sign up for the newsletter. There is a monthly giveaway and when the mood strikes other fun things like deep discounts in the shop.

www.brandywalker.net

facebook.com/BrandyWalkerfanpage

twitter.com/Brandy_W

OTHER BOOKS BY BRANDY WALKER

TEZ PUBLISHING

Tiger Nip

Craving More, Book 1

Claiming More, Book 2

Dallas & Kacie: Tiger Bite, Book 2.5

Finding More, Book 3 (future release)

Giving More, Book 4 (future release)

Seeing More, Book 5 (future release)

Freefall

Caught in the Moment, Book 1

Fly Guy Next Door, Book 2

Captured by Color, Book 3 (future release)

Revving Her Engine, Book 4 (future release)

Spinning Out of Control, Book 5 (future release

Mystic Zodiac

Thane | January | Angel

Parvati | February | God/Goddess

Gideon | March | Shifter

Lisa | April | Nymph (releasing Apr 2015)

Celeste | May | Fae (releasing May 2015)

Willow | June | Witch/Warlock (releasing Jun 2015)

Amber | July | Siren (releasing Jul 2015)

Adrian | August | Dragon (releasing Aug 2015)

Colby | September | Djinn (releasing Sep 2015)

Lucas | October | Vampire (releasing Oct 2015)

Mace | November | Spirit (releasing Nov 2015)

Falcon | December | Demon (releasing Dec 2015)

Keystone Predators

Under Her Spell (releasing Jun 2015)

Praetorian Guards

New series in the works

DECADENT PUBLISHING

ROAR LINE

Shifter U

Shifted Plans, Book 1

Changing Her Tune, Book 2 (future release)